"You deeply resent a lot of things, Harriet—but mainly me!"

His mouth twisted disgustedly before he continued, "Could that be because I'm the one who pointed out your boyfriend's little sideline in blackmail?"

Harrie felt the remaining color drain from her cheeks. "You—"

"I don't think so, Harrie," Quinn whispered grimly as he effectively prevented her hand from slapping the hardness of his cheek.

Harrie was completely unprepared for what happened next. She didn't even have time to avoid Quinn's mouth as it came down to possessively claim hers, his arms moving assuredly about her slender waist as he pulled her body in close to his.

Her limbs had all the response of jelly, knowing she would have fallen if it weren't for the strength of Quinn's arms.

What was she doing?

This man was her enemy!

Quinn had just kissed her. And far from being outraged and disgusted at the unprovoked intimacy, she found that every part of her body seemed to tingle and feel alive....

BACHELOR SISTERS

Meet the Summer sisters:
Harriet, Danielle and Andrea
(or Harrie, Danie and Andie to their friends!).
All three are beautiful, intelligent and successful;
but they've always found their careers more
satisfying than their love lives.... Until now!

The Summer sisters haven't been looking for
love—but then destiny causes Quinn, Jonas and
Adam to cross their paths. Are these exceptional
men going to pop The Question?

Don't miss any of these
fabulous stories by popular Harlequin Presents®
author **CAROLE MORTIMER**!

Carole Mortimer

TO HAVE A HUSBAND

BACHELOR SISTERS

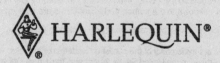

HARLEQUIN®

TORONTO • NEW YORK • LONDON
AMSTERDAM • PARIS • SYDNEY • HAMBURG
STOCKHOLM • ATHENS • TOKYO • MILAN • MADRID
PRAGUE • WARSAW • BUDAPEST • AUCKLAND

My husband, Peter

ISBN 0-373-12188-1

TO HAVE A HUSBAND

First North American Publication 2001.

Printed in U.S.A.

PROLOGUE

'IF I cross your palm with silver, are you going to tell me I'm going to meet a tall, dark, beautiful stranger?'

Harriet's second reaction to this less than respectful remark to her role as Gypsy Rosa, Fortune-teller, was—you *are* a tall, dark, handsome stranger!

It had been her second reaction—because her first had been ouch!

After being stuck in this tent at the Summer Fête most of the afternoon—a typically damp, English June afternoon—these were the first free few minutes she'd had for a much-needed cup of tea. This man walking in here without warning had caused her to spill most of the hot liquid over her hand!

'You *are* Gypsy Rosa, aren't you?' the man prompted mockingly at her lack of reply.

Lord, she hoped so, otherwise her fashion sense badly needed working on! She certainly didn't usually wear flowery skirts that reached to her ankles, or low-necked white blouses designed to reveal rather than hide her cleavage. And her make-up wasn't usually so garish, the red gloss on her lips matching the varnish on her nails. She also wore huge hoop earrings at her lobes, and her hair was completely covered by a bright red scarf.

Her only saving grace, as far as she was concerned, was that the lack of lightning in the closed-in tent, as well as making it stifling hot, also made it impossible for anyone to see her properly, and so recognise her. At least, she hoped it did!

Her sister Andie usually took over this role at the Sum-

mer Fête, and loved every minute of it, but this morning
her sister had woken with the beginnings of flu. Everyone
else, it seemed, already had their role to play at the fête,
and so it had been left to her to—reluctantly—become
Gypsy Rosa.

Until the last few moments, it hadn't been too difficult.
She'd lived in the village most of her life, and knew all
of the people who lived here, so it wasn't too hard to
predict romances, weddings, even births in some cases, and
the rest of what was said she just made up to make it sound
more interesting.

Until the last few moments...

Because even in the subdued lighting of the tent, she
knew she had never seen this man before!

Although she could obviously see he was tall. And dark.
And his physique seemed to imply he was muscular as
well as handsome. He was certainly a stranger, of that she
was sure!

'Please sit,' she invited in the husky voice she had
adopted for her role of Gypsy Rosa, indicating the chair
opposite hers at the table, surreptitiously putting her mug
down on the grass at her feet before wiping her wet hand
on her skirt beneath the table—otherwise she would be
crossing his hand with tea!

Close up she could see him a little better; he had dark
hair and light-coloured eyes, either blue or grey. His face
all hard angles, his chin square and determined, he wore
a dark suit and a white shirt. Well, she could tell one thing
just from looking at him—the way he was dressed, he had
no more expected to be at a village fête this afternoon than
she had expected him to walk into her tent to have his
fortune told!

'It started to rain again,' the man drawled, looking
across at her, his brows raised derisively.

Ah. In other words, he wouldn't be in here at all if he

hadn't needed to step inside out of the rain that had dampened a lot of the afternoon!

She held back a smile at this disclosure: at least he was honest.

'I'm afraid it takes a little more than silver nowadays,' she murmured throatily. 'The board outside tells you it costs a pound.'

'That's inflation for you,' he acknowledged dryly as his hand went into his trouser pocket to pull out a pound coin and place it on the table between them.

'Would you pass it to me, please?' she invited—for what had to be the fiftieth time this afternoon!

It was amazing how many people, even though they knew it wasn't a real 'Gypsy Rosa' inside this tent, still came in here hoping she would tell them some good news. Although it seemed rather sad to her that it appeared to be the lottery most people hoped to win nowadays rather than wishing for anything else good that could possibly happen to them.

He raised his brows even further as he complied with her request, although his mouth twisted mockingly as, instead of taking the money, she took his hand into both of hers to look down intently into his palm.

She knew absolutely nothing about palm-reading, but as the afternoon had progressed she'd realised you really could tell quite a lot about a person from their hands. And this man was no different. For one thing, his hand was quite smooth, meaning he didn't physically work with his hands. It was also his left hand he had brought forward, a left hand bare of rings.

She glanced up at his face beneath lowered lashes. It was a hard, indomitable face, with a touch of ruthlessness if it should prove necessary to his plans.

No, she decided, that lack of a ring did not, in this man's case, mean that he was unmarried; he was just a man who would resist any show of ownership, even that of a wedding ring.

But while he obviously didn't do physical labour with his hand, it was nevertheless a strong hand. The nails were kept deliberately short; if he was a musician he certainly wasn't a guitar player. She remembered quite vividly from her youth having to keep the nails on one hand long so that she could pluck at the guitar strings!

Well, she had decided what he wasn't—now all she had to try and work out was what he was!

Quite honestly, she didn't have a clue. Wealthy, from the cut of his suit, and the silk material of his shirt. And, as she knew from his entrance, he was possessed of a mocking arrogance that spoke of a complete confidence in himself and his capabilities. Wealthy, then, she decided.

But that only made his presence at a small village fête all the more an enigma!

Or did it...?

Perhaps not, if her guess was correct.

She moved further over his hand, frowning down as if in deep thought. 'I see a meeting,' she murmured softly.

'That tall, dark, beautiful stranger?' he taunted mockingly.

She shook her head slowly. 'This is with another man. Although he is a stranger to you,' she continued, frowning. 'This meeting will take place soon. Very soon,' she added as she felt the sudden tension in the hand she held in hers.

'And?' he prompted harshly.

Yes—and? She had worked out by a process of elimination who this man might possibly be, and it seemed from his reaction to what she was saying that she was probably right, but what did she say to him now?

At this moment she felt, with the rain teeming down outside, as if only the two of them existed, that the rest of the world were a long, long way away. It was almost as if—

She blinked dazedly as the tent-flap was thrown back suddenly to admit the light—and a young lady who looked very like a drowned rat at this moment, with her red hair plastered over her face from the deluge of rain still falling outside.

She glared at the man sitting opposite 'Gypsy Rosa'. 'I've been looking everywhere for you,' she muttered accusingly, pushing the wet hair from her face.

The man stood up, smoothly taking his hand back as he did so. 'Well, now you've found me,' he drawled unconcernedly, although his eyes—now identifiable as aqua-blue—were narrowed coldly.

The young woman nodded. 'I've come to take you up to the house.' She indicated the umbrella in her hand—something she obviously hadn't taken the time to use on herself on her run over here! 'If you've finished here, that is?' she added with a derisive twist of her lips.

The man glanced back at 'Gypsy Rosa', those strange-coloured eyes gleaming with mocking humour. 'Yes, I believe I've finished here,' he said dismissively.

They'd barely begun, but as 'Gypsy Rosa' really had nothing else to tell him, perhaps it was as well this particular fortune-telling had been interrupted!

She stood up, holding out his pound coin. 'I believe you're a man who makes his own fortune,' she murmured dryly.

He gave an acknowledging inclination of his head, although he made no effort to take back the money she offered him. 'Keep it to put in the fête's funds; I believe it goes to a good cause.'

A party for the village children, where great fun was had by all. But she was surprised he'd bothered to find that out...

'Thank you.' She dropped the money into the jar with all the other pound coins she'd collected through the afternoon.

He turned back to the young woman standing near the entrance. 'Then I'm ready whenever you are,' he prompted.

The young woman with the red hair nodded tersely, turning outside to put up the umbrella, her impatience barely contained as she waited for the man to precede her out of the tent.

Uh-oh, 'Gypsy Rosa' winced inwardly as she watched the pair hurry across the lawn through the rain to the house. From her sister Danie's behaviour towards him just then he had already done something to upset her this afternoon, and Danie certainly wouldn't have kept that rancour to herself!

Which boded ill for the meeting that was about to take place inside the house...!

Talking of which, it was time that Harriet went back to being herself, and for 'Gypsy Rosa' to retire...

CHAPTER ONE

QUINN'S fingers tapped restlessly on the arm of the chair he sat in. Quite frankly, he was tired of waiting for the arrival of his host for the afternoon, Jerome Summer. Justifiably so, in his book.

He'd been flown in by helicopter to the Summer estate earlier this afternoon. After landing on the smooth lawn that backed onto the impressive manor house, he'd been informed by the pilot that the man he had come here to meet, Jerome Summer, had been called away elsewhere, but would hopefully be back later on this afternoon.

It had been that 'hopefully' that had rankled him the most about that statement. Jerome—Rome—Summer was obviously a busy man, hence this Saturday afternoon appointment in the first place, but Quinn's time was no less valuable, and hanging around at the country fête that was being held on the estate, for most of the afternoon, was not using that time effectively as far as he was concerned.

Besides, it was one of the most boring afternoons he had spent for a very long time!

Well...except for the fortune-teller; she might have proved interesting. But he'd hardly begun to talk to her before being interrupted—by the red-haired virago he was quickly learning to dislike!—with instructions that he was wanted up at the house—now.

Well, he had been up 'at the house' for fifteen minutes now, and Jerome Summer still hadn't put in an appearance. Quinn should have realised that the tea tray waiting for him in the sitting-room was rather ominous!

He would wait for another five minutes, he decided

11

coldly, and then he would ask to be flown back to London. Which wasn't in any way going to help solve the problem he'd come here to talk over with Jerome Summer, but at the same time Quinn refused to be treated offhandedly.

'Ah, my dear Mr McBride, so sorry to have kept you waiting!' greeted a jovial male voice seconds after Quinn had heard the door open behind him.

The man who'd entered the sitting-room was recognisable on sight as his host, Jerome Summer. The man's photograph as often as not adorned the pages of the newspaper Jerome owned, admittedly usually on the financial pages, about one successful business feat or another. He was tall, blond-haired, with a still boyishly handsome face despite his fifty-odd years—those photographs in no way portrayed the sheer power of the man, both physically and charismatically.

He smiled cheerfully as Quinn slowly stood up, holding out his hand in greeting. 'Estate business, I'm afraid,' Rome excused his tardiness dismissively. 'With a place this size, it's never-ending.' He shrugged good-naturedly.

Quinn knew something of the other man; he never liked to meet adversaries without being at least partially briefed. Jerome Summer had bought this estate, comprising the house and extensive grounds, including a deer-park, and half the cottages in the village itself, some twenty years ago. A widower for some years, he now lived here with his three children.

But, as Quinn also knew, those facts only told half the story. Jerome Summer was a self-made man. As the youngest son of a country doctor, he'd built up a financial empire over the last thirty years with various business enterprises, until now, aged fifty-four, he was one of the richest and most powerful men in England. And his complete ease of manner spoke of the confidence that wealth gave him.

It also explained why he'd felt no qualms about keeping

Quinn waiting about for hours; if Jerome Summer was half
the man of shrewdness Quinn guessed him to be beneath
that boyish charm, then *he* would also have done his homework on *him*. The McBride family, of which Quinn was
now the head, chaired and was the major shareholder of
one of the most prestigious banks in London. But it was
a bank with which Jerome Summer had no personal or
business dealings.

'Ah, good, you've been given tea.' Jerome Summer indicated the tea tray on the table.

For all of Jerome Summer's breezy attitude, Quinn was
quite sure the other man was well aware of what his movements had been for the whole afternoon, tea being the last
thing Jerome was interested in!

'It's probably cold by now,' he told the other man dryly
as his host poured tea into the second cup that had been
on the tray when he'd arrived—giving Quinn the hope at
the time that Jerome Summer himself would appear at any
moment!

The other man looked up to grin at him. 'Believe me,
over the years I've become used to drinking tea in all sorts
of guises.' As if to prove his point he straightened to take
a swallow of the lukewarm brew.

Quinn was becoming impatient again. He'd come here
because he had something he needed to talk to this man
about, something of great importance to him, and with this
man acting as if he'd just called in on the off chance of
being offered afternoon tea it was becoming increasingly
difficult to bring the conversation round to what he
wanted—needed!—to talk to Jerome Summer about.

'Mr Summer—'

'Please call me Rome,' the other man invited lightly,
relaxing back in one of the armchairs. 'And do sit down,
dear boy; you're making me nervous towering over me
like that!' He laughed softly up at Quinn as he still stood.

Quinn's eyes narrowed. 'I doubt that very much—Rome,' he bit out tersely, not fooled for a moment by the other man's apparent friendliness. And he certainly wasn't a 'boy', dear or otherwise. At thirty-nine, he'd controlled the McBride Bank for the last ten years, and very successfully too.

The other man continued to smile, giving an inclination of his head. 'Perhaps so,' he drawled in an amused voice. 'But humour me anyway.' He indicated the comfortable chair opposite his own across the coffee-table.

Quinn had an idea that most people humoured this man, for whatever reason. In his own case, he decided as he sat down, it was because the matter he wanted to talk to Jerome Summer about was urgent—and very personal. 'I really do need to talk with you, Rome.' He sat forward in his seat. 'You see—'

'Could you just wait a few more minutes, Quinn?' the other man asked. 'I'm expecting my lawyer to join us at any moment,' he explained at Quinn's frowning look.

Quinn stiffened in his chair. Lawyer? What the hell—?

'I believe I explained to your secretary, when I made this appointment to see you, that this was a private matter?' he bit out harshly. Damn it, he didn't want a lawyer involved in this!

Rome gave another gracious inclination of that leonine head. 'Of course, dear boy, but I've invariably found that the presence of a lawyer is always a good idea—in any situation,' he added hardly, revealing some of the steel Quinn had been sure lay beneath that surface charm.

Quinn's mouth tightened. This was personal, damn it. He didn't want a lawyer present.

'I can assure you that Harrie is the soul of discretion,' Rome added dismissively, bending confidently forward to help himself to one of the sandwiches Quinn had ignored earlier and which were now starting to curl a little at the edges.

Quinn had no doubt that, over the years, discretion was something this man's lawyer had been much in need of! Quinn's expression was grim. He had, he already felt, been jerked around enough by this man for one day. Of course, that had always been the danger when agreeing to meet Rome Summer on his own home ground, but when Quinn had originally been offered this meeting at the Summer estate it had seemed better than no meeting at all. Now he wished he'd tempered his impatience and waited until the other man were free to see him in town. Except, as he inwardly acknowledged, neither he nor Corinne had that time to wait...

Although he'd already learnt enough about this man to know any sign of weakness on his part would quickly be spotted—and as quickly taken advantage of!—by this shrewd adversary.

Quinn drew in a softly controlling breath, deliberately maintaining his own relaxed posture. 'I believe, in this case, you will find you have wasted your lawyer's time,' he drawled dismissively, his own eyes narrowed now, deciding he would hate to play chess with the other man!

Rome Summer shrugged. 'It's my time to waste,' he murmured pleasantly.

'But—' Quinn broke off as he heard the door open behind him, noting the pleasure that lit up the other man's face as he stood up. The shrewdness had gone from Rome Summer's face now as he grinned boyishly before crossing the room to greet the person who had just entered.

'Sorry I'm late; I was unavoidably detained,' murmured a huskily soft voice in apology.

A female voice, Quinn noted with a frown, turning in his chair before slowly standing up to get a better look at the woman who had just entered the room.

Only to find himself looking at the most beautiful woman he'd ever set eyes on!

She had long hair, the colour of midnight, which fell in soft tumbling curls down her back; while long lashes of the same colour surrounded eyes the colour of emeralds, her skin the colour of magnolia, her nose small and pert, covered by a sprinkling of freckles, her mouth wide and smiling, a poutingly sensual mouth, the red lip-gloss she wore a perfect match for the long painted nails on her slenderly expressive hands. She was tall and slender, the tailored grey suit and white blouse she wore adding to that impression of height; her legs were long and shapely beneath the knee-length skirt.

But it wasn't only the woman's obvious beauty that made Quinn stare across the room with narrowed eyes; Rome Summer had grasped both of those slender white hands in his, even as he bent down and kissed one pale magnolia cheek!

Quinn's brows rose knowingly. Obviously—despite their own appointment today!—life wasn't all business for the older man. But as Rome Summer had been a widower for the last ten years, and was obviously still a very attractive as well as powerful man, that wasn't surprising. Quinn just wished the other man's current girlfriend—for this young woman must be almost thirty years younger than Rome Summer—had waited until Quinn had finished his own business with the older man before disrupting their meeting!

Rome put his arm about the woman's slender shoulders as he brought her further into the room, his grin more boyish than ever. 'Come and say hello to Quinn McBride, darling,' he invited softly.

The woman walked like a dream too, Quinn thought contemptuously, her movements fluid while at the same time totally feminine. Sheer perfection, in one five-foot-eight-inch package, Quinn acknowledged grimly. But then, with Rome Summer's wealth, Quinn wouldn't have expected anything less of the current woman in his life!

'Mr McBride,' the woman greeted huskily, standing only inches away from Quinn now.

He found himself looking down at one of those artistically slender hands, at the same time becoming aware of the light headiness of her perfume, a perfume that jolted a memory for him from somewhere, although for the moment he couldn't remember where.

But one thing he was sure of, he'd never met this woman before; she wasn't the sort of woman any man would ever forget once having seen her!

He took the slender hand in the largeness of his own—and almost pulled it away again as quickly!

Something that felt very like an electric shock had passed from the woman's fingers through to his own; a slightly tingling sensation remained in his hand even now, although he resisted the urge to massage away that sensation with his other hand.

His eyes were narrowed to aqua-blue slits now as he looked at the woman for any sign in her own expression that she'd also felt that electrical charge. The gaze that steadily met his own was as cool and impersonal as the jewels they resembled.

Beautiful but cold as ice, Quinn decided, impatiently dismissing his own reaction as he turned to look at Rome Summer once again. 'I have to be back in town by early evening,' he prompted the other man pointedly.

'Of course,' the other man accepted lightly, indicating Quinn should resume his seat. 'Fire away,' he invited cheerfully once they were all seated, Rome having opted now to sit on the sofa beside the young woman.

Quinn gave her a frowning look. Okay, it was a weekend, and the other man obviously had other, more pleasurable plans to occupy his time, but Quinn still had no intention of discussing his private business in the presence of Rome Summer's girlfriend!

'I've already explained to you that my business is private,' he began tautly.

'And I've already assured you—' the other man nodded abruptly '—that anything you say in front of Harrie will be completely confidential.' He looked at Quinn challengingly.

It took tremendous effort of will on Quinn's part— helped by years of running and controlling a worldwide banking concern, where his own tremendous control could mean the difference in millions of pounds for his bank and investors alike—to keep his own expression bland.

Harrie! This woman, obviously an intimate friend of Rome Summer's, was the *lawyer* he'd said would be in on their meeting!

Quinn looked at the woman with fresh eyes, reassessing her businesslike appearance in the tailored suit and blouse, the cool beauty of her face, noting the confidence in her gaze that seemed to say, whatever her private relationship with the older man, she was nevertheless a lawyer, and a damned good one!

Strangely enough, despite her unprofessional intimacy with her employer, Quinn had a feeling she was, too!

He gave an acknowledging inclination of his head. 'This is, nevertheless, a private—very private—matter, to me,' he repeated grimly. 'One that doesn't require legal advice,' he added determinedly.

Not being in control of a situation wasn't something Quinn was particularly comfortable with, and this situation had already been out of control before he'd been made aware of it. Rome Summer, he felt, was the only one now who could put a halt to it in any effective way. If he chose to do so... And Quinn resented having to appeal to this man in the presence of a third party. Especially a third party who, as well as being Rome Summer's lawyer, was obviously the other man's mistress too!

'Quinn—I may call you that, I hope...?' Harrie looked at him enquiringly, the perfect black arc of her left brow raised questioningly.

He gave an acknowledging inclination of his head. 'Mr McBride' might put this meeting on a more formal level, but in the circumstances it was that very formality that he was trying to avoid.

She smiled in acknowledgement of his agreement, her teeth very white and even against the red lip-gloss. 'Then, Quinn, wouldn't it be better if you just told Rome what your problem is, and tried to forget my presence here altogether?' she suggested smoothly.

For one thing, she wasn't the sort of woman any man could easily ignore! 'Just what makes you think I have a "problem"—Harrie?' he bit out, his narrowed gaze levelled on her challengingly.

She blinked once. Just the once. But it was enough to tell Quinn he had briefly disarmed her. But the brief satisfaction he felt at that knowledge was as quickly dispersed as he inwardly admitted there was a problem, even if it wasn't of his own making. But it also made him wonder whether Rome Summer already knew exactly why he'd wanted to see him today... After all, Rome Summer was just as likely to have done his homework on *him* once the appointment had been made!

Harrie shrugged slender shoulders. 'I believe you told Audrey as much when you made this appointment. Rome's secretary,' she explained at his questioning look concerning the mention of the other woman.

He recalled the friendly efficiency of the other woman's voice when he had telephoned Rome Summer's head office yesterday. And, yes, he had told her that. He would never have got this appointment to see Rome Summer so quickly if he hadn't!

But he could also see that, with true legal guardedness, the beautiful Harrie had eluded actually answering his question...

Pompous ass, Harrie thought inwardly, knowing there would be no outward sign of her inner feelings as she continued to look across at Quinn McBride with cool impartiality.

He'd looked at her when she'd entered the room earlier, summed her up, pigeon-holed her as a frothy female friend of Rome's, and as quickly dismissed her as nothing more than an unwanted irritation. Until he'd realised she was Rome's lawyer.

Oh, he'd tried to hide his surprise when Rome had told him of her identity, a polite mask coming down over those handsome features, but it hadn't been quick enough to hide the brief shock that had been reflected in his eyes, the stunned disbelief, before he'd done another mental assessment of her role here today.

Not that his second summing up had been all that complimentary, she acknowledged ruefully; he obviously believed now that Rome was a man who mixed business with pleasure. But at the same time she could see he did accept her legal qualification too!

If he'd known Rome at all, which he obviously didn't, he would have realised the other man never confused his personal life with that of his business one; he may occasionally link them together, but he never, ever confused them...!

Rome had informed her when she'd arrived at the house earlier that this meeting with the banker, Quinn McBride, was planned for this afternoon, and in truth she'd been as puzzled as Quinn McBride obviously was that Rome should require her presence during the meeting. But she hadn't questioned the request in the way that Quinn McBride obviously had; she'd accepted that Rome always had a reason for everything he did.

Quinn McBride finally turned away from her dismissively, his mouth a grim line as he looked across at the older man. 'It appears I have little choice but to accept the situation,' he bit out harshly. 'But I do so on the understanding that what I have to say will be treated as completely confidential, that it is not for discussion with anyone outside of this room. And I do mean *anyone*!'

Harrie bridled with indignation. She was a lawyer, for goodness' sake; of course this conversation would be completely confidential.

'You have my word on it,' Rome drawled derisively, laughter gleaming in his blue eyes as he glanced briefly at Harrie.

Well at least one of them found Quinn McBride's attitude funny—because Harrie certainly didn't! She'd met too many men like Quinn McBride in her years of climbing up the legal ladder, men who took one look at her surface beauty and wrote off any chance of there being a brain under the tumbling black hair. Usually she took great delight in proving those men wrong, to their own detriment, but at the moment this situation with Quinn McBride was a complete unknown to her.

'Mine, too,' she added softly.

Quinn McBride didn't even glance at her this time, his expression grim as he glared down at the cooling teapot. 'My business here today concerns one of the reporters on your newspaper, Rome. And my sister,' he added harshly.

Harrie frowned. Rome owned a newspaper, yes, but she didn't think the minutiae of the lives of the people that worked on it would be of any interest to him. In fact, she was sure of it!

Rome obviously shared her view. 'Let me get this straight. One of the reporters from my newspaper is involved with your sister, and you want me—'

'Certainly not!' Quinn McBride cut in disgustedly. 'My sister is—engaged to marry someone else completely,' he rasped harshly. 'This...reporter—for want of another word,' he added contemptuously, 'has information concerning my sister's past—'

'Something detrimental?' Rome guessed, catching on fast to the other man's angry tone. As he usually did...

It was the key to his success, of course. Outwardly pleasant and amiable, Rome nevertheless possessed a sharp intelligence, and a certain knowledge of his fellow human beings that had saved him from disaster more than once. Anyone who underestimated Rome was heading for disaster.

Although somehow Harrie didn't think Quinn McBride fell into that category; she sensed the quiet respect with which he addressed the older man.

'As you say,' he gave an acknowledging inclination of his head. 'Something detrimental,' he said heavily. 'Not of particular relevance in normal circumstances,' he added firmly. 'But—'

'These aren't "normal circumstances",' Rome finished hardly. 'Am I right in assuming you only have the one sister, Quinn?' Blue eyes were narrowed shrewdly now.

Harrie looked at him thoughtfully, having a definite feeling that he already knew Quinn McBride had only the one sibling...

'Yes,' the other man confirmed abruptly. 'The situation is—delicate, to say the least, and—'

'I can understand your concern, Quinn,' Rome cut in smoothly. 'I just don't know what you want me to do about it. Information, bringing the truth to the general public, is what newspapers are about—'

'I'm not sure I altogether agree with you there,' Quinn scorned derisively. 'The truth, yes. Sensationalism, for the sake of it, no.'

'"...Let them that be without sin themselves cast the first stone" syndrome, hmm?' Rome accepted ruefully.

'Something like that.' Quinn's mouth twisted with distaste. 'I would lay odds on there being very few adults, over the age of say...twenty-five?—who don't have something in their past they would rather weren't made public knowledge!'

Rome nodded. 'And if I were a betting man—which, incidentally, I'm not—I think I would agree with you. How about you, Harrie?' He turned to her enquiringly. 'You're what...? Twenty-nine now? I'm sure there must have been something in your life already that you would rather were kept a secret?'

The conversation had been turned on her so suddenly Harrie didn't even have time to cover up her reaction to the bluntness of the question, her cheeks colouring fiery red under Rome's mocking gaze and Quinn McBride's scornful one.

Nevertheless, she managed to return Rome's challenging gaze. 'I don't believe we were talking about me,' she dismissed coolly.

'Perhaps not,' he conceded in an amused voice before turning back to the other man. 'To get back to the problem of your sister—' he frowned '—I'm not sure I have the right, even when asked as a personal favour to you, Quinn, to actually bury a story that the public may—'

'That's just the point, this reporter isn't—oh, damn!' Quinn McBride stood up impatiently to pace the room. 'You're a father yourself, Rome, I believe?' he prompted irritably.

'Yes...' Rome confirmed guardedly.

'My sister Corinne and I were left parentless fifteen

years ago, when our parents were killed in the crash of the light aircraft they were travelling in. I was twenty-four at the time, but Corinne was only fifteen.' He made the statement in a flat emotionless voice, but it was obvious he'd only achieved this with the passage of time. 'I, naturally, took over the care of my sister—'

'And the Chair of the bank,' Rome added quietly.

Once again Harrie gave him a narrow-eyed look. Just exactly what else did he know about Quinn McBride? The expression on Rome's face was as inscrutable as usual. Meaning he'd no intention of answering that particular question for her, either now or in the future! It was the way he worked, the way he'd always worked—alone!— and he wasn't about to change now.

'And the bank, eventually,' Quinn acknowledged dismissively. 'But that came five years later; at twenty-four I wasn't old enough or experienced enough to take on such a position. And that isn't the point at issue here,' he dismissed impatiently. 'My sister is thirty now, but it's those past tragic circumstances that make me protective of her still.' He sighed. 'I'm sure you know how it is, Rome, that you must feel the same way about your own children.' He grimaced knowingly at the older man.

Rome gave an answering smile. 'Three girls.' He nodded. 'They've given me my fair share of headaches over the years,' he conceded lightly.

Harrie gave him a frowning look beneath lowered dark lashes; he made those 'three daughters' sound like hellions! Something she knew they most certainly were not!

'But a lot of fun and happiness, too,' Rome added affectionately.

'Mmm,' Quinn agreed distractedly, still moving restlessly about the room. 'My sister married five years ago, but unfortunately her husband died of cancer two years later. Corinne was, naturally, devastated,' he murmured heavily. 'She was inconsolable for the first year after Paul died. And then, when she finally felt able to look at the world again, she—she made a mistake,' he added firmly, looking challengingly across the room as he did so.

For her own part, he could have saved himself the trouble, Harrie puzzled thoughtfully; she was no nearer knowing what point he was trying to make than she had been when she'd arrived a few minutes ago for this meeting! Although she very much doubted that Rome, despite his encouragingly friendly expression, was as uninformed...

'It happens to the best of us,' Rome conceded gently.

Quinn McBride's mouth set grimly. 'Not to the woman who is about to marry the MP tipped to be a future prime minister of the country!'

Corinne *Westley*, Harrie suddenly realised dazedly; Quinn's sister was *Corinne Westley*. Up till now she'd been going on the surname McBride, which had totally thrown her, but Corinne's previous marriage now explained that mistake.

Corinne Westley... Tall, beautiful, blonde, elegant, engaged to marry the MP, David Hampton. The wedding was to take place later in the summer, and her photograph, usually at some charity occasion or a political function, appeared in the tabloids nowadays almost as much as the equally elegant and beautiful Princess Diana had once done.

And a reporter working on Rome's newspaper had uncovered some sort of scandal involving the beautiful Corinne that could bring all of that particular castle tumbling to the ground...

No wonder Quinn McBride was worried! Although, in the circumstances, she didn't know what he expected Rome to do about it.

'Why don't you sit down again, Quinn?' Rome invited smoothly. 'I'll have some fresh tea sent in.' He picked up

the telephone and rang down in the kitchen. 'And then you
can explain all this to us quietly and calmly.'

Harrie could see by Quinn McBride's momentarily irritated expression that he was about to argue the point, that
he already considered he was discussing all of this 'quietly
and calmly'! And then he obviously thought better of it,
sitting back in the chair he had so recently vacated, staring
rigidly out of the window as Rome dealt with the ordering
of the fresh pot of tea.

It gave Harrie chance to study the younger man further.
At thirty-nine, he was ten years her senior, but she could
see from the faint sprinkling of grey in the dark hair at his
temples, the lines beside his nose and mouth, that those
ten years hadn't been easy ones. And, from the sound of
it, the reasons for that were understandable; Quinn
McBride had had the onerous burden of responsibility
thrust upon him at a very young age, both for his younger
sister and, even more heavily, as chairman of a bank. His
own youth had probably been put permanently on hold!

She reached out impulsively and lightly touched his arm
as it rested on the side of the chair. 'I'm sure Rome will
help sort this out,' she assured him softly; underneath all
that money and power, she knew that Rome was really a
softie at heart.

Aqua-blue eyes were turned to her glacially. 'Unfortunately, this isn't something that can be "sorted out" by
the gift of a diamond bracelet, or the promise of a weekend
in Paris,' Quinn answered her contemptuously.

Harrie pulled her hand away from his arm so quickly it
was as if she had been burnt. She'd been right about him
earlier; he *did* think she was Rome's mistress. And a very
shallow one at that!

She looked at Quinn with narrowed green eyes, back in
her role of lawyer now, deeply regretting her completely
feminine reaction to his obvious worry concerning his sis-

ter. 'The price of happiness comes a little higher than that nowadays,' she bit out harshly.

Those aqua-blue eyes also narrowed. 'I've heard something similar to that once before today...' he murmured in a puzzled voice.

Harrie's gaze didn't waver. 'If your attitude continues to be as unyielding as it appears to be today, my guess is you're going to hear it a lot more in the future, too!' she told him scornfully.

His mouth thinned angrily. 'I—'

'Tea will be here directly,' Rome put in cheerfully. 'I don't suppose you would like to join us for dinner this evening, Quinn?' he pressed lightly.

Harrie turned to him with accusing eyes. Quinn McBride, despite his obvious genuine love and concern for his sister, was one of the rudest most arrogant men Harrie had ever met—and that was saying something! The last thing she wanted at this moment was the anticipation of having to sit down to dinner with him this evening too!

Quinn's mouth twisted ruefully. 'Perhaps you should wait and hear the rest of what I have to say before making such an invitation,' he drawled mockingly.

Rome laughed softly. 'I doubt that will make the slightest difference,' he assured, obviously enjoying the other man's company despite the gravity of the situation Quinn wanted to discuss with him.

Quinn gave an inclination of his head. 'Nevertheless, I think—'

'Ah, tea,' Rome said with satisfaction as, after the briefest of knocks, the door opened. 'Delivered by the beautiful Audrey, no less!' He smiled his thanks to the other woman as he moved to take the laden tray from her.

Audrey Archer, forty-two years of age, petite and blonde, and undoubtedly beautiful, had been Rome's secretary and assistant for the last twelve years—and her slightly exasperated glance in Rome's direction as he took the tray from her unresisting hands showed she wasn't in the least impressed by his flattery. Flannel, Audrey called it. And she was undoubtedly right!

But at least the light-hearted incident had diverted the attention for a few minutes, giving Harrie time to recover from the insult Quinn McBride had delivered to her without so much as a second's hesitation. He'd obviously summed up not only her, but also what he believed to be the situation between Rome and herself. Pompous ass! she inwardly repeated her earlier summing up of him.

She rejoined the conversation to find that Rome had introduced Audrey to Quinn McBride, but also to hear Rome inform Audrey to tell Cook there would be one more for dinner. Obviously Quinn McBride was staying whether he wanted to or not!

'Leave the number for dinner as it is, Audrey,' she told the other woman pleasantly. 'I have to go back to town in a couple of hours,' she explained at Rome's questioning look.

She noticed there was no such look from Quinn McBride, the mockery of his gaze telling her he knew exactly why she was leaving earlier than obviously expected—and that he was amused by the fact!

Whereas Rome didn't look at all pleased by her change of plan. 'You made no mention of that this morning,' he bit out, giving her a frowning look.

Harrie decided he could frown all he liked; she would not subject herself to any more of Quinn McBride's insulting company than she had to. And for the moment she'd no choice but to sit out the rest of this meeting, but this evening, she considered, was her own time, and she would spend it how she wanted to—and that most assuredly did not include being in Quinn McBride's arrogant company!

She shrugged unconcernedly. 'I'm sure you'll cope without me,' she mocked lightly.

'That's hardly the point,' Rome bit out impatiently. 'You—'

'Andie is feeling a little better now, Rome,' Audrey cut in smoothly. 'I said you would probably pop up later,' she added in parting.

'Half an hour or so,' Rome promised in a pleased voice.

From the abrupt change in Rome's mood at the mention of Andie's recovery, Harrie knew Audrey had succeeded in what she had set out to do—namely divert Rome's displeasure away from Harrie. She turned to give Audrey a grateful smile before the other woman left the room, receiving a conspiratorial one back before Audrey closed the door softly behind her.

But Harrie's smile faded as she turned back to find Quinn McBride watching her with narrowed eyes, obviously well aware of the silent exchange between the two women—and as obviously drawing his own conclusions!

Well, let him; she wasn't answerable to him or anyone else for anything she did or said! Although Rome's next comment wasn't conducive to that impression!

'Would you like to pour the tea while Quinn and I continue our discussion?' he invited distractedly, his thoughts having already returned to the matter in hand. 'You were about to tell us about your sister's "mistake",' he prompted softly.

Quinn McBride looked grim once again. 'I don't think I was about to go that far,' he bit out curtly. 'It's enough that the mistake was made, without going into the details. It's this reporter's reaction to the knowledge of it that is really the point at issue,' he added harshly. 'I—ugh!' He grimaced his distaste after distractedly taking a swallow of the tea Harrie had just poured for him.

In the absence of any preference from him as to how he

liked his tea, Harrie had added milk and two sugars before placing the cup of tea on the table in front of him.

'Too sweet?' she prompted too 'sweetly' herself!

He carefully put the delicate china cup back down onto its matching saucer before turning to look at her. 'For future reference—I do not take sugar in either tea or coffee,' he bit out grimly.

For 'future reference', she had no intention of ever pouring him either brew ever again!

Rome's narrowed gaze in her direction was sternly disapproving, bringing an end to her mental berating of the man who was fast becoming more than just an irritation. 'Please—take mine.' She held out a second, as yet untouched, cup to him. 'And for *your* future reference, I don't take sugar in tea or coffee, either,' she added pleasantly, knowing by his throaty chuckle that Rome, at least, wasn't fooled for a moment by that pleasantness.

'I'll bear that in mind,' Quinn McBride acknowledged dryly before turning back to the older man. 'Did you know that at least one reporter on your newspaper isn't averse to using blackmail in exchange for information?'

Harrie was stunned by the question, although, having come to know a little of Quinn McBride in the last fifteen minutes or so, not nearly so much so by the bluntness with which it was made!

Blackmail...? What on earth was he talking about?

And he'd said this meeting had no legal, or illegal, connotations! The last Harrie had heard, blackmail very definitely came under the heading of the latter!

She glanced at Rome, not fooled for a moment by the calmness of his expression—the angry glitter of his eyes, prompted by the other man's words, told a completely different story!

Rome placed his own cup and saucer back down on the coffee-table before meeting the younger man's accusing gaze with a frown. 'What sort of information?' he pushed hardly.

'Political, what else?' Quinn snapped harshly. 'When this man first approached Corinne with the information he had concerning her past, she believed it had to be the end of her relationship with David, that the last thing he needed to forward his political career was a wife who was going to bring disgrace to his name.' His mouth twisted contemptuously. 'But that isn't what this particular man has in mind at all...' he added grimly.

'Go on,' Rome prompted softly.

Harrie wished he would too. It wasn't too difficult to guess what Corinne Westley's 'mistake' might have been—a young widow, devastated by the premature death of her husband; she'd been prime material for a relationship she hoped might help to ease some of her pain. And, in this case, it sounded as if the partner in that relationship had probably been a married man...

As Rome said, it happened, especially when someone was that vulnerable. And also extremely beautiful.

But that was still no excuse for what seemed to be happening to Corinne Westley now...

Quinn sighed heavily. 'This man believes, as do most of us in the City, that David will eventually become Prime Minister. The price for this reporter's silence is any inside information Corinne can give him on political issues—hoping to make them political scandals!'

After what Quinn McBride had already intimated, this wasn't too difficult to guess. And in view of his closeness to his sister, it was no wonder he was angry about it.

Rome looked just as angry. 'The man's name?' he bit out in that flat, emotionless tone that showed just how angry he really was.

'I have your guarantee that nothing we have said so far

will go any further than this room?' the other man prompted again cautiously.

The guarantee was unnecessary, Harrie knew that; Rome could be determined, even ruthless if the occasion warranted it, but he had never done an underhand thing in his life. And he couldn't abide the characteristic in others. Harrie had no doubt that the reporter's days of working on any newspaper Rome owned, and possibly any others either, were numbered!

She also felt that perhaps Quinn McBride was right, and her presence at this meeting wasn't needed...

'Rome?' she quietly demanded his attention for a moment. 'Perhaps it would be better, after all, if I left you and Mr McBride to finish this conversation in private?'

'You'll stay put,' he rasped harshly, causing Harrie to look at him with puzzlement for his vehemence. 'The man's name?' he prompted Quinn again.

Harrie turned to look at the other man too, knowing there was no point in reasoning with Rome on her own behalf when he was in this mood; 'Rome's inflexible mood', she'd always called it. And it meant literally what it sounded like; generally the most affable and charming of men, Rome was implacable in this mood.

'Richard Heaton,' Quinn told him with distaste.

Harrie's breath caught in her throat, the look she gave Rome now one of silent accusation. Because she could tell by the now calm expression on his face that he wasn't in the least surprised by the name the other man had just given him—because he had already known it!

What else did he know...?

From the fact that he had told her this morning he wanted her presence at this meeting, and the way he'd told her to stay put a few minutes ago, Harrie had the feeling that he 'knew' quite a lot more than he had so far revealed to her.

Most important of all, she was sure that Rome knew of her own relationship with Richard Heaton...

CHAPTER TWO

His visual attention concentrated on Rome Summer, Quinn felt rather than saw the female lawyer's reaction to what he'd just said. She'd stiffened defensively, as if, instead of merely stating the name of the man who was hounding his sister, he had actually personally insulted her.

He turned to her, to find her gaze fixed on Rome Summer, angrily, accusingly.

Quinn shook his head as he turned away, mentally dismissing the woman, and her...relationship, with his host; it was none of his business if she chose to be the plaything of a rich and influential man. He was here to sort out the complex and potentially damaging situation Corinne was caught in the middle of.

'Richard Heaton...' Rome repeated hardly.

Quinn nodded. 'Do you know him?' With all of Rome's business interests, it wouldn't be so surprising if he didn't; efficient as he thought himself, Quinn couldn't claim to know all of his employees, either!

'Not personally, no,' Rome answered curtly. 'But I have heard of him,' he added.

Causing the woman Harrie to give the older man another sharp look, Quinn noticed irritably. Beautiful as she was, he hadn't wanted her here in the first place—and she'd done little since that time to warrant him changing that opinion!

'Really?' she prompted softly now, her emerald gaze narrowed on her employer.

Rome returned that probing gaze unflinchingly. 'Really,' he drawled mockingly. 'Surprised?' he added tauntingly.

34

The woman swallowed noticeably, looking slightly pale, Quinn noted curiously, giving him the definite impression that there was something going on in this conversation that he had no part of. But whatever it was, he, for one, certainly didn't have the time for their games.

'I—'

'Could we get back to the subject?' Quinn rasped his impatience over the top of what Harrie had been about to say.

'The subject being that Richard Heaton is blackmailing your sister into giving him an edge on any political stories she might have access to, both now and in the future, in exchange for not making public her own past indiscretion?' Rome stated bluntly.

This man was as forthright as he was himself, Quinn realised ruefully. But by the same token, he winced inwardly, in this case, a little softening of the truth might have been welcome. After all, it was his sister the two of them were discussing.

'That is a very strong accusation to make, Mr McBride,' Harrie put in coldly. 'Blackmail of this kind is definitely a prosecutable offence. But, by the same token, so is slander. In which case, Mr McBride, I hope that you're sure of your facts?' she asked harshly, staring at him with glittering green eyes.

Quinn realised she was Rome's legal advisor, but, nevertheless, he wished she would stop interrupting! There were only the three of them in the room, for God's sake; who, if it should emerge that what he was telling them wasn't the truth—which it most certainly was!—was going to make that claim of slander?

'I'm very sure of my facts,' he told her with dismissive contempt. 'And I'm hoping that, between the two of us—' he turned back to Rome '—we may be able to do something about it?' It was a question, but at the same time it was also a plea for the other man's help.

Which didn't sit too well on his usually capably independent shoulders, Quinn acknowledged ruefully. Although he had a feeling that Harrie would claim that independence was actually arrogance!

Oh, damn what the woman thought of him, he told himself impatiently. She was beautiful, yes, but she was also the mistress of Rome Summer—which, in his eyes, nullified her legal capabilities in this instance. Even if they should turn out to be excellent. Which was yet to be proved...

'Even if what you claim should turn out to be the truth, exactly what is it you expect Rome to do about the situation?' she persisted in claiming his attention.

Much to Quinn's increasing chagrin! In his experience lawyers were there to advise when asked for that advice, and if not they remained silent until consulted. Rome's personal relationship with this woman had given her an arrogance of her own that was completely intrusive in this particular situation.

Quinn gave her a humourless smile. 'I think that's for Rome and myself to decide—don't you?' he prompted insultingly.

She drew in a sharp breath as that insult registered, turning to her employer. 'I strongly advise you not to become any more deeply involved in this situation until we have had chance to look into it ourselves,' she told Rome stiltedly.

'There's nothing to talk about, darling,' Rome murmured apologetically before turning to Quinn. 'And I believe I already have an idea that may be the solution to your problem.' He stood up to stroll over to the tray of drinks that stood on the dresser. 'Tea is all well and good,' he said lightly, 'but sometimes something a little stronger is required; can I get you a whisky, Quinn?' he offered, holding up the bottle of twelve-year-old malt.

Ordinarily, he would have refused, rarely indulging in the stuff, and never when he was working. But this wasn't work as such, and he *was* invited for dinner...

'Thanks,' he accepted, becoming more convinced by the moment that Rome was going to help him in this situation. 'Just a small one. No ice or water,' he added as he relaxed back in his chair. They were both more than capable men; he was sure that between the two of them—Harrie's aggravating presence excluded!—they could come up with a way to put an end to Corinne's difficulty. They had better; he'd assured his sister that they would!

'Harrie?' Rome offered smoothly.

'No—thank you,' she refused stiffly, her cheeks bright red now where minutes ago they had been unnaturally pale, her hands tightly clasped together on her primly set knees. 'Rome, I really think—'

'I already know what you think, Harrie,' Rome cut in gently, stepping forward to hand Quinn his drink before moving forward and lightly placing his free hand on one of Harrie's tensed shoulders. 'But Quinn is telling the truth, darling,' he murmured huskily. 'He—'

'I don't believe you—or him!' Harrie stood up abruptly, moving away from that restraining hand to include Quinn in her angry glare, her body rigid with fury now as she faced the two of them across the room. 'I simply do not believe Richard is capable of doing the things he has been accused of here today!' she stated coldly, her head raised haughtily.

If anything she was even more beautiful in her anger, Quinn acknowledged abstractly. Totally wrong in her summing up of the situation, of course, but extremely beautiful, her eyes flashing like emeralds, an attractive flush to her cheeks, her breasts pert beneath the tailored suit, her legs long and shapely. Beautiful, and desirable. Although Quinn had never questioned why Rome was involved with her, only the sense of mixing business with pleasure. Even with a woman as beautiful as Harrie...

And the question also remained, why was she so angry?

Although the answer to that seemed to lie in the way she'd claimed Richard wasn't capable of the things he'd been accused of today...

Quinn's eyes narrowed on her, giving her the second reassessment of the afternoon. The first had been when he'd realised she was the lawyer Rome had previously spoken of. The second was the realisation that she knew Richard Heaton. The question was, *how* well did she know him? Well enough to claim his innocence, it seemed.

He looked curiously at the older man, wondering if Rome had already known of Harrie's friendship with the young reporter. Because he certainly couldn't be in any doubt about it now!

'Then you would be wrong, Harrie,' Rome told her sadly. 'I'm afraid Richard Heaton is guilty of everything Quinn has accused him of today. And much more,' he added with distaste. 'Darling, I'm sorry you've had to hear the truth about him in this particular way, but—'

'Now that I definitely don't believe,' she cut in with a bitter laugh. 'You're enjoying every moment of this! How long have you known?' she prompted hardly, eyes narrowed accusingly on the older man.

'Harrie, I'm sure Quinn isn't in the least interested in listening to our personal business—'

'I'm not sure I believe that, either!' She turned to once again include Quinn in her furious glare, scornfully taking in his relaxed pose in the armchair, the partially drunk glass of whisky he held in his hand. 'You've drawn some pretty damning conclusions yourself here this afternoon, Mr McBride,' she told him disgustedly. 'All of which are totally wrong,' she added with satisfaction, a contemptuous twist to her red-painted lips. 'I sincerely hope—for your sake!—that the things you've said about Richard Heaton aren't as erroneous!'

Quinn stiffened in his chair, slowly sitting up straighter, his own eyes narrowed now as he sat forward in his seat. 'That sounds decidedly like a threat...?' he murmured slowly.

She was breathing deeply in her agitation. 'I—'

'Take care, Harrie,' Rome cut in gently. 'Quinn is a guest in my home,' he reminded her softly.

For a few brief moments she continued to glare at the two men, and then with an obvious visible effort, she forced herself to relax, to calm down, although the coldly angry look remained on her beautiful face.

'So he is,' she finally murmured gratingly. 'Fortunately, I'm not—so I'll take this opportunity to remove myself. That way you can continue this character assassination of Richard Heaton without fear of interruption!' she added disgustedly.

'Harrie—'

'Rome,' she came back coldly, bending to pick up the shoulder bag she'd put down earlier.

The older man sighed. 'Will you be back down tomorrow?'

Now Quinn did feel as if he were intruding. The last thing he wanted was to be witness to a man of Rome Summer's wealth and power grovelling apologetically to his mistress—especially when, as far as Quinn could see, the beautiful Harrie was the one who was in the wrong!

Quinn stood up. 'Perhaps I should leave the two of you to talk—'

'That won't be necessary, Mr McBride,' Harrie cut in derisively. 'Rome and I have said all we have to say to each other—for the moment,' she added warningly for

Rome Summer alone. 'And I have no idea when I'll be back, Rome,' she answered him.

'Are you going to Richard Heaton?' the older man demanded gratingly.

Harrie's head went up challengingly. 'And if I am?'

Rome gave an inclination of his head. 'Then I advise you to remember that you agreed the conversation we've had here today would be confidential,' he reminded softly.

Green eyes glittered like twin jewels. 'Now who's the one making threats?'

Rome shrugged. 'That's only your interpretation of what I said, darling.' He sighed. 'I was merely reminding you not to let your personal feelings cloud your professional judgement.'

Harrie gave a humourless laugh. 'Personal feelings?' she echoed scornfully. 'I didn't know I was allowed to have any of those—at least, none that don't include the Summer family! But to set your mind at rest, Rome, I am well aware of my professional obligations to you,' she assured him disgustedly before turning to Quinn. 'Just one more question, Mr McBride...?'

He met her gaze unblinkingly. 'Yes?'

'Going on a hypothetical assumption that the things you've said about Richard are true,' she bit out scornfully, leaving them in no doubt as to what she thought of those accusations, 'isn't his source of this information as much as a danger—to your sister—as you claim Richard could be?'

Bright, Quinn acknowledged appreciatively. Still furiously angry at what he had to say about Richard Heaton, but able to think logically in spite of it.

'His source,' Quinn drawled contemptuously as he thought of Andrew McDonald, the man his sister had so briefly become involved with, 'if they should choose to go to the press themselves with this story, is in a position to lose as much as Corinne.' The other man had a wife and two children who had no idea of his involvement with another woman!

'I see,' Harrie murmured, her gaze narrowed on him consideringly—giving Quinn the distinct impression she knew exactly what sort of threat had been brought to bear on that particular source! 'I won't say it's been nice meeting you, Mr McBride, because—'

'Harrie!' Rome cut in sharply.

She sighed deeply before drawing in a controlling breath, forcing the semblance of a smile onto her lips, although it came out looking more like a grimace, Quinn thought.

This meeting wasn't turning out at all as Quinn had hoped that it would: a conversation with Rome Summer, an agreement or otherwise to the other man helping him with this situation, and then he would be on his way. A personal element on the part of the other man hadn't been part of Quinn's suppositions, certainly not to the extent that the other man's girlfriend obviously had some sort of relationship herself with Richard Heaton! It changed things somewhat, although not, Quinn now had reason to believe, to the point that Rome Summer refused to help him. And Corinne...

'Well, you've had your "meeting" with the "stranger", Mr McBride,' Harrie told him tauntingly. 'Although not with the tall, dark female you obviously hoped it would be! You've also successfully maligned the reputation of a man you obviously haven't even met,' she snapped accusingly. 'I hope you're proud of yourself!' she added disgustedly before striding across the room and closing the door forcefully behind her as she left.

Quinn stared at the closed door slightly dazedly, remembering all too clearly where he'd heard Harrie's words before. At the fête earlier this afternoon... From the gypsy...

But how on earth—?

'I hope you'll excuse my eldest daughter, Quinn,' Rome told him with a heavy sigh. 'I'm afraid she's rather hurt and angry at the moment—mostly with me, I hasten to add!—and that isn't conducive to her remembering her manners!'

Quinn was still recovering from the shock of realising that the only way that Harrie could possibly have known of his teasing conversation with Gypsy Rosa earlier this afternoon was if *she* were the fortune-teller herself!

It took several stunned seconds for him to realise exactly what else Rome had just said.

Daughter…?

Harrie was Rome Summer's *daughter*?

'Your eldest daughter…?' Quinn finally prompted huskily, still blinking dazedly.

It wasn't very often he was disconcerted, but at the moment it had happened twice within a few seconds of each other. It seemed that not only was Harrie the gypsy from this afternoon's fête, but she was also Rome's *daughter*…?

Rome gave a rueful grimace. 'Harriet. But we've always called her Harrie. I had a feeling earlier when you mentioned my children that you had no idea those daughters were actually twenty-nine, twenty-seven and twenty-five respectively,' he murmured proudly.

'Or that Harrie was one of them,' Quinn confirmed distractedly, still trying to come to terms with the true relationship between Rome and the beautiful Harrie.

Father and daughter. Not lover and mistress. As he had assumed. And as Harrie, from her earlier scornful remark, had obviously known he'd assumed!

Hell!

'The eldest,' Rome confirmed again. 'Although not the most fiery, I can assure you,' he added with proud affection.

Quinn shook his head, still trying to come to terms with Harrie's true relationship to Rome. 'The redhead that's been bossing me around most of the afternoon wouldn't happen to be another of them, would she?' He grimaced in a vain hope that he could be wrong.

Rome laughed softly. 'That sounds distinctly like Danie. My middle daughter,' he explained at Quinn's blank expression. 'Andie, the youngest, is upstairs in bed with the flu,' he added with concern.

Although, according to 'the beautiful Audrey', Andie was 'feeling a little better now', Quinn recalled heavily.

Quinn could never remember feeling quite this disconcerted. Not only had the lawyer Harrie turned out to be a woman, but she was also Rome Summer's eldest daughter. No wonder she'd looked at the older man slightly askance when he had admitted his daughters had given him his fair share of headaches!

But Harrie wasn't only female and Rome Summer's daughter, she was also Gypsy Rosa...!

And she was wrong when she claimed he hadn't met his 'tall, dark, beautiful stranger'; Harrie Summer more than fitted that description herself!

She wanted to hit someone! No, not just 'someone'; her father or Quinn McBride would do just fine. More than fine!

She'd wondered at Rome's need for her presence at this meeting with Quinn McBride today; she knew that her father had made it an unwritten policy over the years never to conduct business during the weekend, that this was the time he set aside for his family. But when he'd telephoned her yesterday, to make sure she would definitely be here today, she hadn't questioned the request too deeply, just assumed that he must have had his reasons for wanting her here.

And he'd certainly had those!

Just when and how had he learnt of her relationship with Richard Heaton? That he did know couldn't be in any doubt after the things he had said to her earlier.

'What is it, Harrie?' Audrey prompted concernedly as she came out of the study further down the hallway.

The other woman's concern wasn't too difficult to understand, Harrie acknowledged self-disgustedly as she realised she was still standing outside the sitting-room, her hands clenched into fists at her sides.

She drew in a relaxing breath before replying. 'Just Rome up to his usual games,' she bit out sharply.

Audrey raised blonde brows at her vehemence. 'But I thought it was a business meeting?'

Harrie had been only seventeen when Audrey had first begun to work with Rome, nineteen when her mother had died, and so consequently it had been Audrey whom Harriet had turned to when she'd needed to talk over the usual problems teenagers had as they were growing into adulthood.

It was also no secret between the two women that Rome had been bringing home 'suitable' young men for his daughters' perusal for the last five years, in the hope that one of them might eventually settle down and present him with a grandson! 'Suitable' to Rome, of course—so far none of those men had proved in the least interesting to the three sisters.

'Not those sort of games,' Harrie told the other woman derisively; much as Rome might like to see his daughters settled, even he could never imagine Quinn McBride as a potential son-in-law.

Besides, Harrie was quite capable of picking her own husband, thank you very much. In fact, until a few minutes ago, she had thought she *had* chosen him...

'Come along to the study where we won't be disturbed,'

Audrey invited gently as she read the look of confusion on Harrie's face. 'You can tell me all about it,' she added warmly.

Much as she felt tempted to do exactly that, Harrie knew that she couldn't. For one thing she had given a promise of confidentiality to her father and Quinn McBride. And for another, the whole thing was too painful at the moment to even think of confiding in someone else, even abstractly, any of the things Quinn McBride had accused Richard of.

Not that she believed them. Not for a minute. But she needed time to gather her own thoughts. And to do that she had to get away from here!

'Not today, Audrey.' Harrie reached out and squeezed the other woman's arm in apology. 'I'm so angry with Rome at the moment that I don't even want to run the risk of seeing him again today. Or Quinn McBride,' she added as she remembered the other man was staying for dinner. 'I think it best if I keep to my decision to go back to town.' The sooner the better, as far as she was concerned!

'You know where I am if you change your mind,' Audrey told her encouragingly.

Harrie grimaced. 'Unfortunately, wherever you are, Rome tends to be too!' As her father's personal assistant, Audrey tended to travel all over the world with him. It didn't allow Audrey any personal life of her own, but, as she'd never married, Audrey didn't seem to mind that. 'But there is one thing you could possibly help me with...?' she said slowly, frowning slightly.

Audrey gave her a considering look. 'And what's that?'

She moistened dry lips. 'Has my father ever mentioned a Richard Heaton to you?' she prompted lightly.

Audrey raised blonde brows. 'In what connection?'

'In any connection!' Harrie bit out disgustedly.

The older woman gave a rueful grimace. 'Are you seriously expecting me to answer that?'

Not really, no. Close as she was to the other woman, Harrie had always known that the older woman would never betray Rome's confidence in her, either personally or professionally—just as Audrey would never betray any of the confidences Harrie had given over the years either! In fact, she was being unfair, Harrie realised, to have even asked Audrey such a question.

'Forget I ever asked.' Harrie squeezed the other woman's arm in apology a second time. 'I'll be off in a few minutes,' she added grimly. 'I hope you enjoy dinner this evening!'

Audrey laughed softly at her insincerity. 'I thought Mr McBride looked rather—interesting,' she drawled pointedly.

Harrie's eyes widened in surprise. Audrey had been involved with the Summer family for so long now that Harrie had almost forgotten that the other woman was only in her early forties, and that she was still a very beautiful and desirable woman. In fact, there were only three years' difference in Audrey's age and Quinn McBride's…!

Harrie grimaced. 'If you're partial to snakes!' she acknowledged with feeling. 'Personally, I'm not!'

Audrey chuckled again, blue eyes gleaming with laughter. 'He certainly made an impression on you, didn't he?' she teased.

'With the impact of a brick!' Harrie acknowledged disgustedly. 'I really do have to go,' she added with a pointed look towards the sitting-room; the last thing she wanted was for either man to open the door and find her still standing outside in the hallway!

'Andie will be most upset if you don't go in and see her before you leave,' Audrey warned. 'She's at the feeling-sorry-for-herself stage,' she added affectionately.

Harrie grinned at the description. 'How my little sister hates to be found looking less than her best!'

Audrey shared in the humour. 'She doesn't make the best patient in the world,' she acknowledged ruefully.

That was definitely an understatement, Harrie realised after sitting with her disgruntled youngest sister for five minutes, glad to have the excuse of returning to town as a means of making good her escape.

Although she didn't make that escape quite as she had hoped...!

Just as she reached the bottom of the wide staircase the sitting-room door opened and her father and Quinn McBride stepped out into the hallway.

Harrie gave them both a coldly dismissive glare before turning sharply on her heel and walking briskly across the wide hallway to the front door.

Was Quinn McBride now aware that she was Rome's daughter and not his mistress, as he had so obviously assumed earlier? Probably, she accepted with satisfaction. Not that she expected the other man would feel in the least uncomfortable about his erroneous assumptions; he had the look of a man who very rarely regretted any of his actions!

'Harrie!' her father called to her impatiently even as she wrenched the huge oak door open.

She froze, drawing in several controlling breaths before slowly turning back to face him. 'Yes?' She deliberately kept her attention centred on her father, patently ignoring Quinn McBride, a fact she was sure he was well aware of. And probably amused by!

Which only made her angrier than ever. There was nothing even remotely funny about this situation. Even if she could prove that the accusations Quinn McBride had made, concerning Richard, were all lies, she would still have to convince her father of that. And, as all of his daughters knew only too well, underneath that happily unconcerned persona Rome had a will of steel!

'I only wanted to ask you to drive carefully, darling,' her father told her gently.

She should have known! She'd been expecting admonition for her earlier behavior—she knew that she hadn't heard the last of that!—and instead Rome had totally thrown her by being her loving, caring parent. And he had done it on purpose. Damn him!

'I always do,' she assured him dryly, turning stiltedly to Quinn McBride. 'I hope you enjoy your weekend, Mr McBride,' she told him contemptuously.

He raised dark brows at her obvious sarcasm. 'I doubt I'll be able to do that, not when I seem to have ruined yours!'

Harrie's eye flashed deeply green at his presumption in believing anything he had to say could affect her one way or another. 'Not in the least,' she assured him scathingly, chin raised defiantly. 'What you had to say this afternoon was interesting, but, as I'm sure Rome can confirm, I stopped believing in fairly tales a long time ago!'

His mouth tightened at the intended insult. 'I'm sorry you feel that way,' he said softly. 'Maybe if you met my sister, talked to her, you would feel differently...?'

Harrie gave him an outraged glare. 'I doubt that very much,' she bit out dismissively.

Meet Corinne Westley! Tall, blonde, beautifully composed Corinne Westley? Quinn McBride's sister? That was the last thing Harrie wanted.

No...the last thing she wanted was to stand here and continue this conversation with Quinn McBride!

She turned to her father. 'I really do have to go now,' she told him abruptly. 'I'll be in the office on Monday, as usual,' she assured him dryly, knowing her father was quite capable of coming in search of her if she didn't arrive at work as usual on Monday morning.

She'd intended becoming a junior partner in a law firm

after obtaining her legal qualifications, but her father had persuaded her to work for him for a few weeks. And the weeks had turned into months, the months into years, until she was well and truly ensconced in handling all the legalities of her father's business dealings.

It had been an easy option, she realised now, and maybe it was time she moved on. Besides, she wasn't sure she could continue to work for, and with, her father after what had happened this weekend...

'Harrie...?' Her father frowned at her.

'Rome,' she returned unhelpfully, meeting his gaze challengingly.

Her father was too astute, that was his problem—because he had, she was sure, picked up on some of the thoughts that had been going haphazardly through her mind! Well, he wasn't going to know about any of them until she'd worked out in her own mind exactly what she was going to do.

His mouth tightened disapprovingly. 'We'll talk on Monday,' he muttered grimly.

'We certainly will,' she agreed lightly.

And she knew exactly what she was going to say to him too!

'Once again, I wish you both a happy weekend,' she added hardly.

'Er—actually, Harrie, Quinn has decided to take a rain check on dinner this evening,' her father told her dismissively. 'I thought you must have already left—'

'I've been up to see Andie,' Harrie told him distractedly, sure her father couldn't really be about to make the suggestion she sensed that he was!

Her father's expression brightened. 'How is she?'

Harrie shrugged. 'Improving, as Audrey told you earlier.'

He nodded his satisfaction with this news. 'I'll go up

and see her myself soon,' he murmured. 'I was actually just about to make the arrangements for Quinn to get back up to town, but as you're on your way back there, anyway—'

'You can't be serious!' Harrie interrupted him scathingly, absolutely horrified at the idea of spending the next hour in Quinn McBride's company. And to add insult to injury, in the confines of her own car!

'If you wouldn't mind?' Quinn McBride put in softly.

Her eyes flashed as she turned to glare at him. 'And if I do?'

'Harrie!' her father remonstrated exasperatedly.

'It's all right, Rome,' Quinn McBride assured him soothingly. 'I'm sure Harrie has her reasons for feeling the way that she does.' He turned back to her. 'The drive into London will give us an opportunity to talk. I feel that you need to hear more about my sister's—dilemma, before you get back to town,' he added as Harrie would have interrupted once again.

Before going back and telling Richard of his accusations, was what Quinn really meant, Harrie knew. Well, she had given her word that she wouldn't do that, it was a promise she wouldn't break. But that didn't mean she couldn't leave Quinn McBride guessing. In her opinion, it was the least he deserved!

She gave him a humourless smile. 'I don't think I need to hear any more than I already have, Mr McBride,' she told him tauntingly. 'And I'm equally as sure you have no more wish to spend any more time in my company than I do in yours!' she said disgustedly.

'True,' Quinn McBride acknowledged dryly. 'However, I do believe we need to talk,' he added hardly.

And she knew exactly what they 'needed' to talk about. Well, he was going to be out of luck if he thought she would discuss Richard with him—because she most certainly would not. The man had come here and made horrendous accusations about the man she loved; there was no way anything he chose to say to her in private could change that.

She gave a deep sigh. 'You're wasting your time, Mr McBride,' she told him tightly. 'But I am leaving now— if you're ready to go?' she invited ungraciously.

His mouth quirked into a rueful smile. 'I've had politer invitations—but,' he continued firmly as she would have interrupted, 'in the circumstances, I accept.'

Harrie didn't need to be told what circumstances they were! But if he wanted to spend an unpleasant hour in her company, while she drove them both back to London, that was completely up to him.

'I'll see you on Monday, Rome,' she told her father dismissively as she opened the door to leave.

He nodded distractedly. 'I'll call you later, Quinn,' he told the other man with a frown. 'As soon as I have everything arranged,' he added grimly.

Harrie shot her father a sharp look at this enigmatic remark, but she could read nothing from his expression.

Damn him.

Damn *both* of them!

Exactly what were the two of them up to? Because she had the distinct impression Rome had told Quinn McBride his idea for a solution to his sister's problem—and received Quinn McBride's agreement to it!

She had the next hour to try and find out what that solution was!

CHAPTER THREE

QUINN wasn't so sure, when he found himself seated in Harrie Summer's car a few minutes later, that he had won this particular point!

He watched Harrie beneath lowered lids as he sat beside her in the Jaguar sports car. It was a car definitely not built for the comfort of a man six foot three inches tall; the seat had to be all the way back to accommodate the length of his legs, the back of the seat tilted back too in an effort not to have his head tilted sideways against the cabriolet roof!

Not that Harrie had the same problem, he acknowledged ruefully. She seemed perfectly comfortable in the low leather seat as she sat behind the steering wheel, and there were several inches to spare above the darkness of her hair.

He also had no doubt she was well aware of his physical discomfort as she accelerated down the gravel driveway away from the house, a smile of grim satisfaction curving those red-painted lips.

It was probably the least he deserved, he realised heavily, after the blow he had so obviously dealt her this afternoon. It might be one she might ultimately thank him for, he considered grimly, but at the moment she most certainly didn't feel that way!

To his surprise, he found he wasn't in the least worried about Harrie Summer telling her boyfriend what had been said about him this afternoon. At least...not too much; he believed he knew enough about human nature to recognise that Harrie Summer was a woman of principle, that she'd made a promise, and that she would stick to it. Even if it should cause her emotional pain to do so.

That it *had* caused her emotional pain to hear the things he had said about Richard Heaton, he didn't doubt. He'd seen the pain he had caused reflected in those expressive green eyes. And he felt a complete heel for being the one to tell her damning things concerning someone she obviously cared about. And, to his surprise, he found he didn't like that feeling at all...!

His mouth twisted at the irony of the situation. At thirty-nine, he had never even lived with a woman, let alone contemplated marrying one; he'd never cared enough one way or the other to make either commitment. Oh, there had been women in his life, sometimes for several months at a time, but they hadn't been relationships he ever thought of taking further than dinner and going to bed together. Now he found he felt more about the fact that he'd hurt Harrie Summer than he'd ever cared about the feelings of the women he'd shared relationships with.

What the hell did that mean?

Harrie Summer was beautiful, yes, and he hated the thought of being the cause of the pain in those gorgeous green eyes, but as for anything else...! Hell, the woman hated him!

Besides, he knew damn well he wouldn't be sitting beside her in this car at all—uncomfortable as it might be!— if it weren't for the fact she believed she could use this time to find out exactly what he and Rome intended doing about Richard Heaton's threats! He'd seen the shrewd look in those expressive eyes when Rome had mentioned telephoning him later, and one thing he was very quickly learning—Harrie Summer was no fool. She was, in fact, every inch her father's daughter!

He turned to her. 'I believe I owe you an apology,' he told her softly, seeing the start of surprise she quickly brought under control, instantly knowing she had misunderstood the reason for his apology. 'For the inaccurate "conclusions" I drew this afternoon,' he explained dryly.

She gave him a scathing glance. 'So Rome explained that I'm his daughter.' She shrugged dismissively.

'And not his girlfriend? Yes.' Quinn nodded self-derisively. 'Although I have the feeling *he* hadn't realised I ever thought you were anything else!' He winced.

Harrie grimaced. 'Rome just assumes everyone knows who his daughters are.'

'Whereas you aren't so naive?' Quinn turned slightly in his seat so that he might see her better, that perfume he had savoured on her earlier making him feel almost light-headed in the close confines of the car.

Gypsy Rosa's perfume...

This woman was an enigma, one moment the perfect gypsy in a fair booth, the next a super-efficient lawyer, then supposed mistress of a rich and powerful man, but in truth the daughter of that same man. No woman had ever intrigued him as much as Harrie Summer did, Quinn realised a little dazedly.

Again she turned to give him a cursory glance. 'I recognise a cynic when I meet one,' she said scornfully.

A cynic, yes; he'd been that for some years, Quinn recognised dismissively. But when faced with men like the blackmailing Richard Heaton, and the weak Andrew McDonald, was that so surprising? Although, Quinn realised, Harrie was accusing him of another type of cynicism altogether...

He shrugged. 'Rome forgot to mention the relationship between the two of you either before or after he introduced us.'

Harrie gave a scathing laugh. 'And on that basis you decided I was his mistress?'

'He did call you darling,' Quinn reminded lightly. 'Several times.'

'He called Audrey beautiful—but she isn't his mistress, either!' Harrie told him disgustedly. 'But as my mother has been dead for over ten years now, and Rome is very much a man, I have no doubt there have been and still are, women in his life.' She frowned. 'He is just very discreet about any relationships like that he might have. He certainly never brings any of those women to the family home,' she added dismissively.

Quinn smiled. 'No doubt that's because he was thinking of the moral welfare of his three daughters!'

Harrie shot him a look of intense irritation. 'Don't patronise me, Mr McBride—'

'The name is Quinn,' he interrupted softly. 'And I wasn't being patronising,' he added frowningly. 'Rome is obviously a very doting father, takes an avid interest in all of you.' And the fact that all three daughters had been present on the summer estate this weekend showed that Rome had a very good relationship with all of his daughters. A least, he *had* had. Quinn winced again...

'Yes,' she acknowledged heavily. 'Sometimes too much so,' she added hardly.

Quinn had a feeling that she considered her relationship with Richard Heaton was one of those occasions! Well if he were the father of three daughters—heaven forbid!—he had no doubt he would feel equally as protective. No matter how adult and in charge of their own lives they might feel they were!

'Harrie—'

'Quinn—'

They had both begun talking at once, breaking off at the same time too. Quinn looked enquiringly at Harrie now as he waited for her to finish what she had been about to say.

She gave a heavy sigh. 'You, like my father, have obviously realised that Richard Heaton is a personal friend of mine…?'

Of course he'd realised that. And, 'like her father', he wasn't happy about it. But for a totally different reason, he realised slowly. Rome just didn't want one of his much-loved daughters involved with a man as unscrupulous as Richard Heaton obviously was. Whereas Quinn found he didn't like the idea of Harrie being involved with any man…!

He gave her a narrow-eyed look. As he had noted several times before today, Harrie was a very beautiful woman. But she was lots of other things too…

Obviously, despite their slight argument earlier, she was a loving daughter to Rome, as well as being an efficient legal advisor to him. She also seemed to have a warm relationship with Rome's female assistant, as well as apparently having a close relationship with her sisters. Lastly, she was loyal to her friends, even when those friends—especially in the instance of Richard Heaton!—didn't deserve that loyalty. Harrie Summer, Quinn decided, was a person it was all too easy to like. And respect.

It was a pity that she couldn't stand the sight of him…!

'It has occurred to me,' he drawled lazily.

Harrie gave him an impatient glance for his inappropriate levity. 'Then it must also have occurred to you,' she bit out tauntingly, 'that I'm not going to simply stand by and see you and my father hurt him, or his career?'

That had seemed a distinct possibility, yes. 'You made a promise to your father,' Quinn reminded tightly.

Her mouth tightened stubbornly. 'That I wouldn't tell Richard any of our conversation today, yes,' she acknowledged coldly.

'But…?' Quinn prompted warily.

'But that doesn't prevent me from trying to find out for

myself if what you said is the truth,' she told him challengingly.

It was no more than he had expected. No less than he would do himself if the positions were reversed. But by the same token, he couldn't allow Harrie to upset any of the plans he and Rome had made today.

'And if it is?' Quinn did some challenging of his own.

She drew in a ragged breath, obviously not pleased at the suggestion. 'Once I know all of the facts, I'll know the answer to that question, too,' she told him determinedly.

That loyalty was indeed very strong. Or was it something much deeper than that? Could Harrie Summer actually believe herself to be in love with Richard Heaton?

'Would you have dinner with me when we get back to town?' Quinn suddenly heard himself say.

And then sat back in surprise as he considered his own invitation. That he was intrigued by this woman wasn't in doubt. That he found her attractive, both physically and mentally, also wasn't in doubt. But was this really the time for him to be suggesting the two of them had dinner together?

The answer to that question was an unequivocal no! He was leaving himself open to the biggest verbal slap in the face he had ever received in his life!

The stunned silence that followed showed him that Harrie was as surprised by his invitation as he was at having made it. Well, he mused inwardly, at least she hadn't laughed in his face!

In fact, the silence went on for so long he wondered if he had achieved the impossible—and actually struck Harrie Summer dumb! She certainly had enough to say earlier, most of it to his detriment!

'Hey, it was only an invitation to dinner, not an indecent proposal!' he finally mocked.

Her mouth twisted scathingly. 'It wouldn't have taken

me this long to answer if it had been the latter!' she scorned. 'Okay, Quinn, I'll have dinner with you,' she finally decided firmly. 'But on one condition...'

It took Quinn several seconds to take in her acceptance, but a mere split second to consider the 'conditions'. 'There is no way I'm going to agree not to discuss Richard Heaton,' he warned grimly.

'That isn't the condition,' she assured him harshly. 'I'll have dinner with you only if I'm allowed to pay my half of the bill!'

Considering his previous imaginings over 'conditions', this seemed quite mild in comparison. Although, on reflection, perhaps not... Going halves on the cost of their meal implied some sort of business arrangement—and, while Harrie might consider him to be exactly that, his own intentions towards Harrie Summer, he was quickly discovering, were not of a business nature!

'Fair enough,' he conceded lightly, deciding they could sort that sort of detail out later—once they were safely at the restaurant. 'In that case, perhaps you would like to choose where we eat?' he suggested brightly.

He didn't consider for a moment that Harrie had accepted his invitation because she had any real wish to spend time in his company. No, he'd been all too aware of the determination in her eyes when she'd assured him she wasn't about to ask for his agreement not to talk about Richard Heaton. Harrie's sole intention in having dinner with him at all *was* to talk about Richard Heaton!

'We can telephone from my home to book a table—I just need to go back there and deal with a few things before we go out,' he added as she would have protested.

Harrie's mouth firmed. 'Very well,' she finally conceded tightly. 'I could do with freshening up myself before we go on to the restaurant, anyway.'

In other words, she was only agreeing to that arrange-

ment because it suited her too, Quinn acknowledged, ruefully. Amongst the other attributes he had mentally acknowledged to her earlier, Quinn now added stubbornness.
Harrie wasn't about to concede an inch where he was concerned. And, in the circumstances, he couldn't blame her.

Oh, well, he mused as he relaxed back in the leather car
seat, 'Rome'—excuse the pun!— 'wasn't built in a day'!
and persuading Harrie to see him as a man, and not a
harbinger of bad news, was probably going to take as long
as building that city had done!

And in the meantime, he was happy enough to just sit
silently beside her now that he had her agreement to go
home with him, admiring the way she handled the powerful car. Just admiring her, actually!

But he could see that Harrie was surprised at the detached house, set in its own grounds, that he directed her
to once they reached London. No doubt she'd expected
him to live in an apartment, clinically clean and charac-
terless. But his home was nothing like that; instead it was
a gracious Victorian-style house, surrounded by beautifully
kept gardens.

It was the McBride family home, of course. It had been
his grandparents', and then parents' home, long before it
had become his. And it was a home he took pride in; he
did the majority of the gardening by himself, the hours he
spent outside usually his only form of physical exercise,
as well as allowing him to be mentally at peace with himself.

'Nice house,' Harrie murmured grudgingly as she got
out of the car to join him on the gravel driveway.

Quinn bit his bottom lip to stop himself from smiling at
the ungraciously made compliment. Instead he gave an acknowledging inclination of his head. 'I think so,' he said
dryly, taking a light hold of her arm as the two of them
strolled across to the front door.

And it was a hold he knew Harrie deeply resented as he was able to feel that resentment emanating from every pore of her stiffly held body. It was perhaps as well that she was a well-brought-up young lady, otherwise he might have found himself with his face slapped, after all, for taking even that liberty!

Although, somehow, as he unlocked the front door to allow them to enter the brightly lit hallway he had a feeling that might still be a possibility! One thing he'd learnt about Harrie this afternoon; she didn't like being manipulated into a situation, even by her father—and Quinn was about to do the same thing, major style!

He tensed as the door opened to the left of them in the entrance hall, looking at Harrie now and not at the woman who came out of what he knew to be the sitting-room, seeing the way those green eyes widened with surprise, and then recognition—seconds before she turned to look up at him accusingly...

Corinne Westley!

The woman stepping gracefully into the hallway was instantly recognisable as the fiancée of David Hampton, MP. The sister of Quinn McBride!

He had tricked her, Harrie instantly realised, the invitation to dinner all a ruse just so that Quinn could achieve his purpose. He'd said earlier that he wanted her to know more about his sister's side of things, and the problem she was facing because of Richard—a suggestion Harrie had no qualms in refusing!—only to have Quinn neatly arrange for her to actually meet his sister.

She hadn't wanted to have dinner with Quinn this evening in the first place; she'd only accepted because she'd thought she might be able to get some more information out of him. It had also occurred to her that she might be able to delay things a little if she could ensure Quinn wasn't at home to take her father's call this evening...

And instead Quinn had turned the tables on her, only bringing her here, she was sure, so that she could meet his sister.

Corinne Westley, absolutely beautiful in a fitted black dress, her blonde hair loose about her shoulders, nevertheless looked as disturbed by the encounter as Harrie felt, confusion in those aqua-blue eyes, so like her brother's, as she returned Harrie's narrowed gaze.

Damn Quinn McBride, Harrie inwardly muttered.

Corinne looked as gorgeous as she did in her photographs, but there was also a natural warmth about her, a curving generosity to her peach-coloured lips. There was also a glow of love in her eyes as she looked trustingly at her older brother, a glow that seemed to say—she didn't know who this woman was, or why he had brought her here, but she had complete confidence in the fact that Quinn would never do anything that would hurt her.

Harrie wished she could say the same where her own feelings were concerned!

'I wasn't expecting you back yet, Quinn.' Corinne Westley looked searchingly at her brother, even her voice attractive, pitched huskily low, hinting at a warm sensuality to her nature.

And the reason for her searching gaze was obvious to Harrie; the older woman knew exactly where Quinn had been this afternoon, and for what purpose—and she was anxious to know its outcome!

'Change of plans,' Quinn answered dismissively. 'Shall we all go into the sitting-room?' he suggested lightly, retaining his grip on Harrie's arm as she stiffened slightly. 'I'm sure we will all be more comfortable in there,' he added firmly.

In truth, although Harrie deeply resented Quinn's duplicity in getting her here to meet Corinne, she was now wondering exactly how he was going to explain *her* presence to his sister. Obviously Corinne's problem was a very personal one, one she definitely did not want to become public; how was Quinn going to get around the fact that Harrie knew about it too...?

'Please, sit down.' Quinn indicated one of several chairs in the graciously furnished but comfortable sitting-room. 'A glass of white wine?' he offered once the two women had sat down—in opposite chairs, almost as if Corinne Westley already sensed Harrie was not sympathetic to her 'problem'!—moving towards the drinks cabinet, taking a bottle of chilled wine from the refrigerator.

Harrie was aware of Corinne watching her guardedly from across the room as Quinn poured the wine, keeping her own expression deliberately bland, still waiting for Quinn to explain away her presence. If he did! From the little she had come to know about him this afternoon, Quinn didn't appear to be a man who felt he had to explain himself to anyone! But surely his sister was different...?

'Harrie, this is my sister, Corinne; she lives here with me,' Quinn explained softly as he handed Harrie a glass of white wine. 'Corinne, this is Harrie Summer; Rome Summer's daughter—but also his legal advisor,' he told his sister gently after her start of surprise at Harrie's identity.

Very neatly done, Harrie inwardly acknowledged with grudging admiration. Quinn deliberately hadn't mentioned she was also a friend of Richard Heaton's!

But, then, how could he, when his sister was sure to have an aversion to anything and anyone involved with Richard? Nevertheless, Harrie could still appreciate Quinn's adeptness in overcoming a situation that had, to Harrie, had all the indications of having disaster written all over it.

'You may just have missed your true calling in life, Quinn,' she murmured derisively. 'I think you would have made a good lawyer yourself!' she added as he raised his brows questioningly.

He folded his length down into the chair next to her before answering. 'Strangely enough,' he drawled softly, aqua-blue gaze gently laughing at her, 'I do have a degree in law.'

She should have known! Quinn had been so sure of himself this afternoon, so definite in how far he could and couldn't go. Although Harrie also accepted that the problem Quinn was faced with at the moment, that his sister was faced with, wasn't particularly helped by his knowledge of the law...

'It's all right, Corinne,' Quinn hastened to assure his sister as she looked far from comforted by his explanation of Harrie's presence.

The other woman would have been even less comforted by Harrie's real reason for being here, Harrie decided ruefully.

'Harrie's on our side,' Quinn told his sister firmly, shooting Harrie a warning look as she gave an indignant gasp. 'Rome has agreed to help us, and, understandably, Harrie merely wants to satisfy herself that it's done legally.'

'Harrie' wanted to 'satisfy herself' of a damn sight more than that, her flashing green gaze told him warningly.

Although outwardly she said nothing. She'd taken the opportunity the last few minutes to study Corinne Westley, and it was obvious to even the casual observer—which Harrie certainly wasn't!—that the other woman was so tense she looked as if she might snap, a look of deep strain beside her eyes and mouth, her hands moving restlessly once she'd put her untouched glass of wine down on the coffee-table in front of her. Corinne Westley had the look of a woman who had come to the end of her emotional endurance, as if the least little thing could send her hurtling over the edge...

But could Harrie really bring herself to believe that Richard—tall, handsome, fun-loving Richard—with the alleged threats of blackmail, was the cause of Corinne Westley's undoubted pain...?

Harrie was no longer sure what the truth of the matter was. Quinn seemed to think that Richard was guilty. Her father believed that he was, too. Only she, it seemed, was in the minority. And couldn't that simply be because she was emotionally involved with Richard herself?

Harrie simply didn't know any more...!

Corinne swallowed hard, shaking her head. 'I've done a lot of thinking today, Quinn.' She sighed wearily. 'And perhaps the easiest thing, after all, is if I just bow quietly out of David's life—'

'No!'

To Harrie's surprise she found she was the one who had stepped in with the objection!

But even as she realised that, she realised something else too; Corinne Westley really was as lovely as her photographs, both inside and out—why else would she be suggesting giving up the man she loved just so that something she'd done in the past shouldn't endanger his future political career?

Corinne gave her a quizzical look. 'I appreciate your— concern,' she murmured, obviously puzzled by Harrie's vehemence, 'but, in the circumstances, I can't see any other way out.' She shook her head, her hair a silky blonde cloud about her shoulders. 'If I just fade out of David's life—'

'Do you really think you'll be allowed to do that?' Again Harrie was the one to interrupt her. 'If—if this man is serious in his intention of blackmailing you into colluding with him, with the threat of bringing an end to David's career—'

'Oh, he's serious!' Corinne gave a shiver of revulsion. 'He left me in no doubt about that!'

It pained Harrie to hear Richard talked of in this way. Just as it had pained her a few seconds ago to even suggest that Richard might actually be guilty of attempting to blackmail this vulnerable woman!

She drew in a controlling breath. 'Then you have to realise he could just go ahead and write the story, anyway.' Write it, because after this afternoon Harrie was in no doubt that it wouldn't be her father's newspaper that would print it. But, as she also knew, there were other, less principled newspaper owners and editors who would snap up such a scandalous story. 'Which would damage David's career whether you were still in his life or not,' she added flatly. 'After all, it's a well-known fact that the two of you are supposed to marry this summer.'

'Harrie is right, Corinne.' Quinn spoke for the first time for some minutes, having seemed content until now to sit back and let the two women continue the conversation.

Because he knew, damn him, that once Harrie had talked with his sister, seen the emotional state Corinne was obviously in, she would find it more and more difficult to believe in Richard's innocence!

Well, she *did* still believe in it, Harrie decided firmly— wouldn't stop believing in it until she had heard it from Richard's own lips that he was guilty of their accusations. Although how she was actually to achieve that she didn't have any idea. To actually ask Richard outright if it was true was tantamount to accusing him of the crime. But, by the same token, until she was absolutely sure he wasn't guilty, there was no way she could be her normal loving self with him. She was the loser, it seemed, whichever way she went...

Damn Quinn McBride, she thought vehemently—and not for the first time!

'David is going to be here in a few minutes,' Corinne choked emotionally. 'We're going out to dinner,' she explained. 'I had intended telling him then that our engagement was at an end—'

'For the wrong reason,' Harrie cut in firmly. 'I realise all of this is a strain on you,' she added gently, just how much of a strain it was on the other woman becoming more and more apparent as the minutes passed, 'but I advise you to give it a little more time.'

'I agree with Harrie,' Quinn put in softly. 'Just a few more days, Corinne,' he encouraged. 'A week at the most.'

Harrie gave him a sharp look. Just what plan had he and her father hatched between them this afternoon? The implacable expression on Quinn's face as he calmly returned her gaze told her she wouldn't get an answer to that question from him. And after the way she'd parted from her father earlier today, she didn't think he would be too forthcoming, either!

Richard, it seemed, was her only avenue of information...

She put down her untouched glass of white wine, standing up. 'Time I was going, I believe,' Harrie said lightly, deliberately avoiding Quinn's suddenly sharp gaze. 'I've already taken up enough of your evening,' she told the other woman gently. 'And I'm sure the two of you must have things you want to talk about,' she added hardly, knowing there were definitely 'things' Quinn would like to talk to his sister about—and that he couldn't do so until Harrie left! 'I hope, if we ever meet again, Corinne—' she gave a rueful grimace of a smile at the unlikelihood of that ever happening '—that it will be under more pleasant circumstances.'

'I hope so, too.' Corinne's air of fragility seemed even

more pronounced as she stood up, the skin seeming almost translucent now on the gaunt lines of her cheeks.

No wonder Quinn had been so full of anger this afternoon, Harrie accepted heavily; she would be as protectively furious herself if one of her sisters had been made this unhappy by a third party!

The problem Harrie had had earlier, and still had, was believing Richard was the cause of this woman's heartache...

'I thought the two of us were having dinner together this evening?' Quinn didn't allow her to escape that easily, standing up so that he towered dominantly over the two women.

Harrie felt the slight flush in her cheeks. 'Let's take a rain check on that, hmm? I can see you have other priorities at the moment,' she added quickly before he would have voiced his objections to her leaving a second time.

'I—' Quinn broke off as the doorbell rang. 'That will be David,' he realised grimly. 'Corinne, you are not to do anything stupid, do you hear?' he prompted forcefully even as he moved across the room to answer the door.

His sister gave a pained frown, before slowly nodding her agreement. 'It's just becoming so difficult to keep up this pretence with David,' she groaned.

'You aren't pretending with David,' Quinn told her determinedly. 'You love him. And he loves you. And for the moment that's all you have to think about. The rest of it will sort itself out in time.'

Harrie's heart ached for the other woman as they heard Quinn open the front door, the sound of male laughter, and then the two men talking easily together as they walked down the hallway towards the sitting-room.

'Quinn is right, you know,' Harrie felt compelled to reassure the other woman. 'All that really matters is that you and David love each other.'

Corinne gave her a grateful smile before turning to greet her fiancé, her face raised invitingly for his kiss.

Quinn quirked dark brows across at Harrie as the two of them were witness to the other couple's greeting, the vibrantly handsome MP obviously as in love with Corinne as she was with him, her blue eyes filled with loving pride as David looked down at her, his arm possessively about her slender shoulders as he turned to look at Harrie with politely questioning eyes.

Harrie was completely unprepared for the way Quinn stepped forward to put his arm as possessively about her shoulders, grinning across at the other man. 'You obviously need no introduction, David,' he drawled mockingly. 'And this is Harrie Summer. A good friend of mine,' he added enigmatically.

And Harrie didn't at all care for his method of introduction! Obviously, in the circumstances, it was a little difficult to introduce her as anything else, but she was neither 'a good friend', nor 'his'!

'Pleased to meet you, Harrie.' David shook her hand warmly, a self-assured man in his mid-thirties, with the natural charm of a born leader.

Harrie wasn't 'pleased' about any of this. She hadn't wanted to meet Corinne, let alone her political fiancé, certainly didn't want to witness how happy they were together. But as she glanced at Quinn she could see the satisfied smile that curved those arrogant lips.

Damn him! He had known exactly what he was doing by bringing her here, he'd known just how tenuous he would make her belief in Richard by introducing her to the other couple!

Harrie moved firmly but pointedly away from the weight of Quinn's arm about her shoulders. 'We had just agreed to take a rain check,' she reminded him lightly, avoiding meeting those compelling aqua-blue eyes as she knew they hadn't 'agreed' any such thing! 'Nice meeting you, Corinne, Mr Hampton,' she told the couple politely—if inaccurately; meeting Corinne Westley and David Hampton had been the last thing she'd wanted to do!

'I'll walk you to the door,' Quinn bit out tautly, his displeasure obvious.

To Harrie, at least; the other couple seemed totally absorbed in each other as she preceded Quinn out into the hallway. She felt an ache in her chest at Corinne and David's obvious happiness in each other, waiting only until the door had closed behind them before turning angrily on Quinn. 'You planned that!' she accused heatedly, her hands clenched at her sides.

'Yes, I did.' He gave a challenging inclination of his head.

'But why?' Harrie cried. But she already knew the answer to that! And it was working, damn him...!

Part of her so wanted to see Richard, to establish for herself what was fact and what was fiction. But another part of her was quickly becoming afraid to know that truth...

'You know why, Harrie,' Quinn told her bluntly, eyes narrowed on the paleness of her face. 'Richard Heaton is a blackmailing bastard, and the sooner you accept that—'

'You have no right!' Harrie cut in hotly.

'I have every right,' Quinn assured her grimly. 'You've seen what he's done to my sister; I'm not going to stand by while he does the same thing to you!'

She gasped. 'Richard wouldn't— He couldn't—'

'Couldn't he? You've never confided your secrets to him?' Quinn taunted, his fingers digging painfully into her upper arms as he shook her slightly. 'Pillow talk, I believe it's called. It's what lovers do after they've made love,' he derided scornfully. 'A word here, a confidence there, and before you know it someone's privacy has been compromised. In this case, probably your father's,' he added grimly.

'I never discuss other people with Richard!' Harrie defended indignantly. And there had been no 'pillow talk'! Yet... But she knew their relationship had been well on the way to that intimacy. 'In, or out, of bed,' she bit out furiously. 'And I deeply resent your inference that I would breach my client's—in this case, my father's—confidence!'

Quinn's mouth twisted tauntingly. 'You "deeply resent" a lot of things, Harrie—but mainly me!' His mouth twisted disgustedly. 'Could that be because I'm the one who pointed out your boyfriend's little sideline in blackmail?'

Harrie felt the remaining colour drain from her cheeks. 'You—'

'I don't think so, Harrie,' Quinn whispered grimly as he effectively prevented her hand from slapping the hardness of his cheek.

Harrie was completely unprepared for what happened next. She didn't even have time to avoid Quinn's mouth as it came down to possessively claim hers, his arms moving assuredly about her slender waist as he pulled her body in close to his.

She couldn't breathe, couldn't move, could only feel the crashing assault of Quinn's lips on hers, his hands caressing the slenderness of her back.

This is what drowning must feel like, she decided in the small part of her brain that hadn't been numbed by the demanding kiss. She felt total helplessness to a force that was much stronger than she was, her limbs having all the response of jelly, knowing she would have fallen if it weren't for the strength of Quinn's arms.

What was she *doing*?

This man was her enemy!

And yet…

Quinn slowly lifted his head, his eyes brightly blue as he looked down at her, his expression wary as his gaze moved searchingly across her face.

Harrie could only stare back at him. Quinn McBride had just kissed her, and, far from being outraged and disgusted at the unprovoked intimacy, she found that every part of her body seemed to tingle, and feel alive with—

With what?

Harrie wasn't sure. She had never felt this way before, and couldn't define it. She wasn't sure she wanted to!

She pulled firmly out of Quinn's arms, and stepped back, relieved to find her legs supported her after all, although her lips, when she ran her tongue across their moist warmth, still seemed to tingle from their contact with Quinn's.

What on earth had happened to her just now? She was twenty-nine years old, she'd certainly been kissed before, and believed herself to be in love with Richard.

Believed…?

She *was* in love with Richard!

Her eyes sparkled brightly as she glared up at Quinn. 'I wouldn't advise you to ever try doing that again,' she grated between clenched teeth. 'Not unless you want to find yourself kneed in a very vulnerable place!'

Quinn gave a humourless smile as he held up his hand defensively. 'I've never been into pain,' he drawled mockingly, seeming unmoved himself by the intimate kiss they had just shared.

Because they had 'shared' it, Harrie realised with inner mortification. She had definitely responded to the passionate demand of Quinn's lips, lips she now found her gaze lingering on as she saw his mouth was slightly swollen from the force of their kiss.

Were her lips swollen too? It felt so as she once again ran her tongue over them.

'I would advise *you* not to do that again—unless you want me to repeat the kiss!' Quinn grated harshly, his gaze fixed on the movements of her tongue.

'You know I—' Harrie broke off as the telephone on the hall table begin to ring. 'No doubt that's my father—for you!' she scorned knowingly, green gaze glittering accusingly.

Quinn's mouth twisted derisively. 'Well, it could hardly be for you, now, could it?' he mocked dryly.

Harrie gave a disgusted shake of her head. 'I'll leave you to take your call.' She turned on her heel and walked away, wrenching the front door open to close it decisively behind her.

But a part of her so wished she hadn't had to, that she could have stayed while Quinn took his call from her father...

CHAPTER FOUR

QUINN sighed frustratedly as the front door closed behind Harrie, knowing there was no point in him running after her. For one thing she was in no state of mind at the moment to listen to anything he might have to say. And for another—he had never run after a woman in his life!

And the damned telephone kept ringing incessantly, the noise seeming to jar on his nerve-endings, so that he couldn't even think straight!

He snatched up the receiver, growling a response to the unwelcome caller.

Rome Summer chuckled on the other end of the line. 'I gather you had an interesting drive back to town with my daughter?' he drawled tauntingly.

Quinn felt some of the tension leave his body at the other man's unmistakable mockery. 'That's one way of putting it,' he confirmed dryly, thinking back to the kiss he and Harrie had just shared. But even if he felt like telling Rome about that—which he most assuredly didn't!—he doubted her father would believe it had ever happened.

He had a problem believing that himself! He'd expected Harrie to pull away from him and attempt to slap his face again, but instead she had melted in his arms, not exactly responding—at least, not in the way he'd wanted her to respond!—but not fighting him, either.

Rome chuckled again. 'No one has ever accused any of my daughters of being boring!'

Quinn couldn't give an opinion about the indisposed

Andie, but the red-haired Danie certainly wasn't lacking in self-confidence, and as for Harrie—!

His mouth tightened as he pushed thoughts of Harrie from his mind. 'I hope you have some positive news for me, Rome?' he prompted harshly.

'Very.' Rome instantly sobered. 'I've set the interview up for ten o'clock tomorrow morning. Is that going to fit in with things your end?'

'I'll make sure that it does,' Quinn assured him grimly. 'I just hope that this is going to work!'

'Have a bit more faith, Quinn,' the other man advised. 'You and I both know this is the only way to go with this.'

Yes, Quinn did know that. All he had to do was convince Corinne it was the right way to go, too!

All?

His sister was falling apart in front of his eyes, he realised with a frown. His only consolation was that he knew Harrie had recognised that too. He was also aware she hadn't liked him for showing her that, but if it made her think again about Richard Heaton he could live with that.

Besides, he had every intention of seeing Harrie Summer again...

'I'm sure you're right, Rome. And thanks,' he added gruffly. 'I owe you one.'

'I don't conduct business in that way, Quinn,' the older man came back firmly. 'But thanks for the offer.'

Quinn had liked Rome Summer when he'd finally met him this afternoon, but as time passed he found himself liking and respecting the other man even more. He was rare amongst his breed: a successful man who didn't trample over other people to get where he wanted to go, a compassionate man too, who detested anyone who could threaten a woman. For whatever purpose.

Although, admittedly, in this particular case, Rome's dislike of Richard Heaton probably also stemmed from the fact that he was involved with Rome's beloved eldest daughter!

Which begged the question: would Rome feel quite so kindly towards Quinn, and be quite this helpful, if he were to realise what his own intentions were towards that same beloved daughter? Somehow Quinn doubted it!

Although, as he heard his sister and David in the sitting-room preparing to leave for dinner, he knew he had something much more pressing to deal with. 'I'm the one who's indebted to you, Rome. And somehow thanks doesn't seem enough,' he added with a frown. 'I'll be in touch,' he told the older man quickly in parting, turning to face the other couple as they came out into the hallway.

'What is it?' Corinne was instantly sensitive to his change of mood, frowning at him apprehensively. 'Who was that on the telephone?' she added worriedly.

Quinn's mouth tightened, his eyes becoming glacial as he thought of the man who had brought his sister to this state. He was going to take extreme pleasure in one day beating Richard Heaton to a pulp.

Although, even as he came to that grim decision, he knew that part of his own anger towards the other man was also because of his involvement with Harrie...

He was jealous, damn it.

And it wasn't an emotion he'd ever felt over a woman before. Over anything, he realised frowningly. His family had always been wealthy, ensuring that he and Corinne had an indulged childhood. And there had been nothing, and no one, in his adult life that he couldn't have had if he'd shown the inclination.

But the thought of Harrie going to Richard Heaton this evening, which Quinn was positive she was going to do, filled him with a rage that was also completely out of character.

'Quinn?' Corinne looked at him searchingly.

He shook his head, dismissing—for the moment!—his haphazard thoughts of Harrie. He needed time, and privacy, to try and understand the feelings she evoked in him, and that was something he didn't have at the moment.

'I told you it's going to be okay, Corinne,' he assured his sister gently. 'But before we straighten the situation out, you have to sit down and tell David what happened—'

'I can't do that!' Corinne gasped, giving her fiancé an apprehensive glance.

'Don't be silly, Corinne,' Quinn dismissed briskly. 'David is thirty-five years old, and, I'm sure, no innocent himself.' He gave his future brother-in-law a rueful grin before his face tightened into grim lines. 'And tomorrow we're going to sort out Richard Heaton, once and for all time!' he promised his sister grimly.

'Richard Heaton?' David looked puzzled by their conversation. 'I seem to know that name from somewhere…?' He frowned.

'Corinne will explain over dinner—yes, you *will*,' Quinn told his sister firmly as she would have protested once again. 'It's as well if David knows. And you did nothing wrong,' he added decisively. 'You—' he broke off as the doorbell rang, frowning slightly. 'Are you expecting anyone else this evening?' he prompted his sister even as he moved to answer the door, freezing in the doorway as he saw who stood there.

Harrie!

A bedraggled and very wet Harrie, the darkness of her hair flattened against her head, the business suit she wore damply out of shape too.

'I—'

'Don't say anything, Quinn!' she warned fiercely, her hands clenched at her sides. 'The last thing I need at the moment is one of your sarcastic comments. It must be obvious, even to an arrogant, ill-mannered—'

'I believe the two of you were just leaving?' Quinn turned to Corinne and David standing in the hallway behind him, David, at least, trying to hold back a smile at Harrie's vehement outburst, Corinne looking nonplussed at the exchange.

Exchange? So far Quinn hadn't been able to get a word in edgeways! Although, he had to admit, the fact that Harrie was still here, for whatever reason, brought a grin to his own lips.

'We were.' David was the one to quickly answer him as he saw Harrie's anger at the smile Quinn was unable to contain, and was on the point of another outburst. 'Come on, darling.' David took a firm hold on Corinne's arm. 'I believe Harrie and Quinn want to be alone,' he added dryly. 'And don't worry about a thing, Quinn.' David sobered as he reached his side. 'Corinne will always be safe with me.'

Quinn gave an acknowledging inclination of his head in the other man's direction, knowing that David had received the message in the conversation Quinn had had primarily with Corinne a few minutes ago, and that David would cooperate, no matter what the problem.

He had approved of David Hampton as a husband for his sister from the evening he'd been first introduced to him, and it felt good to know he hadn't been wrong in his judgement.

'Would you stop grinning to yourself in that self-satisfied way—and invite me in out of this damned rain?' Harrie prompted waspishly.

Corinne and David had left while Quinn had been still lost in thought and Harrie, he realised, beautifully outraged Harrie, was wetter than ever!

'Of course.' He stepped back to allow her inside out of the rain that was falling heavier than before, and he was slightly damp himself now as she brushed lightly against him.

Quinn had no idea what she was still doing here, and no clue as to the reason why she had come back to the house. It certainly wasn't so that he could kiss her again! But he was glad that she had. For one thing, it meant she wasn't with Richard Heaton...

'I'm sorry to have interrupted the rest of your evening,' she said stiffly, obviously most unhappy at being here at all. 'But I had to—'

'You have to get out of that damp jacket,' Quinn cut in firmly as he saw she was shivering in the wet clothing. 'Come back into the sitting-room and I'll put the fire on to warm you up,' he invited briskly, already walking back in that direction. 'A brandy might not go amiss, either,' he added as he saw, in the brighter lighting of the sitting-room, exactly how wet she was.

Not only was her hair flattened to her head, but she had water streaming off the silky ends, droplets of rain on her cheeks and eyelashes.

'Why the hell didn't you get into your car out of the rain?' he prompted harshly as he poured them both a glass of brandy, knowing he didn't need his because he was wet and cold, but he had a feeling he might be in need of it, for one reason or another, before this evening was over!

Harrie had bent down over the coffee-table, straightening now, a bunch of keys in her hand. 'Because I left these here earlier!' she bit out impatiently.

Quinn frowned. 'But you must have realised that as soon as you got outside...?'

'Of course I did.' Her face was flushed now, her expression flustered. 'And don't ask why I didn't come straight back and get them,' she snapped as he would have done exactly that. 'You know damn well why I had no wish to come back here!' She glared across the room at him. 'I had actually started to walk back to my apartment, with the intention of collecting my spare set of keys, and then decided that I was being ridiculous when you had a set in here,' she admitted awkwardly.

Which explained why she was so wet, Quinn acknowledged. Although he couldn't say he cared much for the fact that initially she had preferred getting wet through rather than facing him again...!

'Here.' He thrust one of the glasses of brandy out towards her. 'And take that damned jacket off—before *you* catch pneumonia and your father blames me for it!' he snapped irritably.

Harrie took the glass, sipping at the fiery liquid. 'He's more likely to think Andie gave it to me,' she assured him ruefully as she slipped the jacket off her shoulders and placed it over a chair, a little natural colour—as opposed to her earlier anger!—back in her cheeks now as the brandy began to warm her inside.

Quinn's attention was riveted on the cream blouse beneath the jacket. The rain had penetrated right through the jacket, dampening her blouse too, revealing—all too noticeably!—that she wore no bra beneath the silky material, her breasts pert, the nipples a darker pink against the creaminess of her skin.

Hell!

Quinn could never remember feeling aroused when looking at a fully dressed woman before, but the little he could see of the perfection of Harrie's body was enough to send desire surging through his body.

'Sit next to the fire and get warm,' he ordered harshly, dropping down into one of the armchairs himself before the betraying arousal of his own body totally embarrassed him.

Temper flashed briefly in Harrie's eyes as she took obvious exception to his tone, making no move to sit in the chair nearest to the fire. Making no move to sit at all...

'I only came back for my car keys,' she reminded impatiently.

'I wouldn't even send a dog back outside until the rain abates a little,' Quinn rasped insultingly, annoyed with himself for reacting to this woman like some naive schoolboy.

Harrie was beautiful, yes, but she was also opinionated and stubborn, too—too much so for comfort. And he may want her with a fierceness that was becoming stronger by the minute, but what also became more apparent, by those same minutes, was the fact that she didn't even like being in the same room as him!

'Then it's as well I'm not one, isn't it?' she bit out dismissively as she put down the still full glass of brandy before reaching for her jacket. 'Was that my father on the telephone earlier?' she questioned casually as she put the damp jacket back on.

Quinn stiffened warily. 'And if it was?' His eyes were narrowed suspiciously.

Harrie shrugged. 'The plot thickens.'

His mouth twisted mockingly. 'Wouldn't you like to know what he had to say?'

Her cheeks became flushed again, this time with irritation. 'I very much doubt you would tell me if I asked...?'

'Your assumption would be correct.' Quinn gave a mocking inclination of his head.

'Then I won't waste my breath by doing so,' she snapped dismissively. 'Once again, Quinn—'

'I know, it's not been nice knowing me,' he finished dryly, standing up. 'Which is a pity—because I've very much enjoyed knowing you,' he added throatily.

Her mouth tightened as she easily read the double edge

to his words. 'You'll never "know" me, Quinn,' she scorned.

'Pity,' he drawled again. 'But might I suggest that, instead of running straight from here to Richard Heaton's arms,' he continued tautly, 'you go home first and take a hot shower and put some dry clothes on.'

Harrie's mouth tightened resentfully. 'If I ever need your advice, Quinn—for anything!—I'll ask for it!'

He gave a rueful grimace at the deliberate snub. 'I'll come and visit you in your sickbed,' he taunted.

'Don't bother,' she flashed. 'And don't bother to see me out, either,' she snapped as he would have done exactly that. 'I know the way!'

He gave a mocking inclination of his head. 'You should do,' he murmured derisively, seeing the twin spots of angry colour in her cheeks at his deliberate mockery of the fact that she had walked out on him, not once, but twice, this evening!

Harrie gave him a disgusted look, before tossing back her rapidly drying dark hair and turning on her heel to march out of the room, with the front door closing forcefully behind her—for the second time this evening!—a few seconds later.

Quinn's breath left him in a sigh. Part of him wanted to shake her for her mistaken loyalty to a man like Richard Heaton, and another part of him just wanted to kiss her senseless!

Which, in the circumstances, probably made him as much of a fool as he considered her to be...

Rude.

Arrogant.

Opinionated.

Opportunist!

She simply couldn't think of enough expletives to de-

scribe Quinn McBride, Harrie decided on the drive home.
And not just because he had kissed her... Although, she
had to admit, that certainly contributed to the anger she
felt towards him. So much so that she couldn't even force
herself to be pleasant to him long enough to try to find out
exactly what plot he and her father had hatched between
them.

Which was a pity—because, despite what Quinn had
said, she had every intention of speaking to Richard this
evening!

A frown creased her brow as she thought of seeing
Richard. Which was ridiculous. They had been going out
together for several months now, and their dates had always been something she looked forward to, as she found
Richard charming and intelligent. But this weekend had
certainly put a shadow over the relationship.

Quinn McBride had put a shadow over the relationship!

Well, damn Quinn McBride! And damn her father too,
if he had gone into collusion with the other man—which
he certainly seemed to have done.

Once again she wondered exactly what it was the two
men had planned. Damn it, she should have held her temper, should have— But she couldn't, Harrie acknowledged
with a groan, not when Quinn kissed her in that way!

She'd thought him rather cold and calculating at the
Summer Fête this afternoon, a man who rarely thought on
impulse, and certainly never acted on it. But that kiss, she
was sure, hadn't been planned, Quinn had seemed as taken
aback by their reaction to each other as she'd been.
Because, much as she disliked Quinn McBride, Harrie
knew she had responded to him...

How could that be?

Admittedly, Quinn was an attractive man, tall and pow-
erfully built, his arrogance a challenge rather than a put-

off. But she didn't like the man; she found him irritating and presumptuous.

She had *kissed* him, damn it!

Harrie groaned low in her throat at the memory, relieved to see she reached her apartment building, passing through the security gate to the private car park beneath the building, hurrying up to her penthouse apartment on the tenth floor, determined not to give herself any more time to think of Quinn McBride and that kiss they had shared. She picked up the telephone receiver and punched in Richard's number from memory.

But before the number had chance to ring she slammed the receiver back down on its cradle!

What was she going to say to him?

She slumped down into the armchair beside the telephone, putting her head into her hands. Between them, her father and Quinn had shaken her trust in Richard.

Maybe her father, a man she'd loved and trusted all her life, should be able to do that, but Quinn McBride too...?

No...!

Certainly not!

She snatched up the receiver again, pressing the repeat button, her heart beating erratically as the number rang and rang. Richard wasn't at home, she finally accepted heavily.

Of course, she'd told him she would be at her father's estate all weekend, so she couldn't exactly complain when Richard decided to go out for the evening rather than being on his own. After all, he wasn't to know she would change her plans and come back to town—

'Yes?' The receiver had finally been picked up the other end, Richard's voice terse with irritation.

'Richard!' she returned thankfully, her pleasure at finding him at home after all reflected in her voice.

'Harrie...?' He sounded surprised now. 'I didn't expect

to hear from you until you got back to town tomorrow evening.'

As Richard was an employee of her father's, the two of them had decided it might be as well if they kept their relationship to themselves for a while, hence the fact that Harrie never called Richard when she was with her father.

Although, from her father's comments earlier today, they might just as well have saved themselves the trouble; Rome knew about the relationship anyway!

'Change of plan,' she told Richard lightly. 'I'm back in town now, and wondered if you would like to have dinner?'

It was an invitation she had made a dozen or so times before; their free time, because of work commitments, was often limited. But for some reason Harrie felt uncomfortable making the invitation this time, and she wasn't sure whether the hesitant pause on the other end of the line was real or imagined.

Damn, damn, damn!

She didn't even feel her customary ease with Richard now. She seemed to be looking for—looking for what? Guilt?

'Where did you have in mind?' Richard returned huskily.

She *had* imagined that pause! This was Richard, damn it, the man who could make her laugh, who talked to her as an intellectual equal, the two of them sharing many heated debates about the law and politics—

Politics…?

Richard had been very anti David Hampton's political party during one of those conversations, Harrie remembered with a sick feeling in the pit of her stomach, and not too complimentary about the man himself either, now she thought about it.

She gave an inward sigh. It seemed she was questioning

Richard's integrity herself now, which was something she had never thought she would do. She'd always admired his dedication to his work, and believed his articles to be informative and well written.

And nothing had really happened to change that! Okay, so Quinn McBride had come to her father with some wild tale of blackmail, and her father, disliking Richard as he disliked many of the men she chose to go out with, had been easily swayed into believing it. But that didn't mean she had to fall into the same trap!

'I'm sure we'll be able to get a table at Bradleys,' she named a favourite restaurant of theirs, determined to put Quinn McBride's accusations out of her mind. To put the man himself completely from her mind!

'Great,' Richard enthused. 'I'll meet you there in half—no, better make that an hour,' he corrected lightly. 'I need to shower and change first.'

So did she, Harrie accepted as she began to shiver once they had ended their call, peeling off the damp clothing before going into the bathroom to run a steaming-hot shower.

Her father and Quinn were wrong, she decided determinedly as she soaped herself beneath the hot water. Richard was warm and caring, as well as being handsome and intelligent. And it would take a lot to convince her otherwise.

It would take more than Quinn McBride to convince her otherwise!

Although she felt her resolve shaken a little when she was shown to the table at Bradley's shortly before nine o'clock, only to spot Corinne Westley and David Hampton seated at another table across the room!

Not that the other couple were aware of her entrance as they were deeply engrossed in each other, and their con-

versation. About Richard, no doubt, Harrie decided scornfully.

Oh, God, Richard! He would be arriving here himself
in the next few minutes. And even if Harrie didn't believe
the things that had been said about Richard, Corinne
Westley certainly did; how was the beautiful Corinne going to react to seeing him here?

And with Harrie, of all people!

Well, she was going to find out the answer to that soon
enough, she realised with a sickening jolt of her stomach,
as Richard had just arrived at the restaurant and was even
now being shown to their table...!

'It's great to see you!' Richard bent down to kiss Harrie
lightly on the lips before sitting down opposite her at the
table, neither of them into great displays of emotion in
public. 'And so unexpectedly, too,' he added warmly.

Harrie found herself studying him in a way she never
had before, admiring his blonde, boyish good looks, his
body lithe and fit, despite his thirty-four years. He was
looking relaxed and comfortable in a lightweight dark blue
suit and lighter blue shirt, the latter matching the sky-blue
colour of his eyes.

And not the greenish-blue, aqua colour of Quinn
McBride's eyes...

Quinn McBride again! *He* was the reason she was looking at Richard so critically in the first place!

Well, she needn't have worried; Richard hadn't turned
into a two-headed monster since she'd last seen him two
evenings ago. In fact, he looked just as relaxed and charming as usual.

But that didn't stop Harrie giving Corinne and David a
surreptitious glance across the restaurant, heaving an inward sigh of relief as she saw they were still totally engrossed in each other, and had no idea Richard was in the
room. Or Harrie, either, for that matter...

'You seem a little—preoccupied, this evening?' Richard prompted lightly as he noticed her distraction.

Harrie turned back with a guilty start. The last thing she wanted was for him to see the direction of that 'preoccupation'! 'I think I'm catching a cold,' she excused awkwardly, thinking no such thing, having just said the first thing that came into her head. But also having noted, thankfully, that Corinne and David were already at the coffee stage of their meal; hopefully they would be leaving soon. It couldn't be soon enough as far as Harrie was concerned!

Richard reached out and lightly touched her hand. 'Are you sure you feel up to dinner?' He frowned. 'You're looking very pale,' he explained at her questioning look.

'I'll be fine.' She gave him a bright smile. 'And you're right, this is unexpected,' she answered his initial comment. 'I haven't disrupted your own evening, though, have I?'

Richard grimaced, sitting back in his seat. 'The story I'm working on at the moment just isn't coming together; I was glad of the chance to walk away from it for a while!'

'Oh?' Harrie prompted lightly. 'Anything you can talk to me about?'

What was she doing? Richard never discussed his work with her until it was actually in print, so why was she asking him to do so now? She knew why, damn it, and once again she cursed Quinn McBride for being the one to put these suspicions concerning Richard into her mind.

Richard gave a regretful shake of his head. 'You know how it is, Harrie,' he excused ruefully.

'Yes, I know how it is,' she echoed flatly. 'I—' She broke off as she saw that it was Richard's attention that was diverted this time, and, following the line of his narrowed gaze, she could clearly see the reason for it...

Corinne Westley and David Hampton were leaving the restaurant!

Harrie turned sharply back to Richard, her breath catching in her throat as she saw the tension in his body, the calculated hardness of his gaze as he still watched the other couple, the slightly scornful twist to his mouth at the obvious warm intimacy between the two of them.

She was imagining Richard's response to seeing Corinne and David! Looking for signs of recognition!

No, she wasn't, Harrie realised with an inward groan...

There was something about Richard at this moment that reminded her of a satisfied cat that had just lapped up the cream, that same self-satisfied smugness.

A certain knowledge of Corinne that gave him that smugness?

Now Harrie really did feel ill. And it had nothing to do with an imaginary cold!

She swallowed hard once Corinne and David had left the restaurant—thankfully without having seen either her or Richard! 'Do you know them?' she prompted Richard lightly.

The hardness was gone from his gaze now as he turned back to Harrie, giving a dismissive shrug of his shoulders. 'Doesn't everyone?' he drawled derisively. 'The Beautiful Corinne, and the Handsome David!' The scorn could be heard in his voice now. 'But, no, I can't say I know either of them personally.' Richard shook his head.

Harrie didn't believe him. And it had nothing at all to do with the things Quinn McBride had said about Richard, or what her father had intimated, either. She had come to know Richard rather well herself in the last few months, and she also had a lawyer's eye and ear for the truth—and at this moment she knew Richard was lying to her.

Could Quinn's story of blackmail be true, after all? *Was* Richard really capable of that?

Harrie didn't really know. From watching Richard's own reaction on seeing Corinne and David, she felt uncertain enough about it right now not to feel like spending the rest of this particular evening in his company!

She gave a shaky smile. 'I think perhaps you're right about dinner this evening,' she murmured huskily, standing up unsteadily, unable to actually meet Richard's gaze now, needing time—and space—to assimilate her thoughts. 'Suddenly, I don't feel very well at all.' And if she didn't get out of here in a minute, she was actually going to be physically ill!

Richard stood up too. 'I'll drive you home—'

'No! Er, no,' she refused less sharply. 'I can get a taxi—'

'You most certainly won't,' he told her firmly, taking a grip of her arm, making their excuses to the *maitre d'* as they left.

Harrie huddled miserably on her side of the car on the short drive to her apartment. This had been a terrible day, the worst day of her life—and she had no doubt Quinn McBride was to blame for that!

'Shall I come up with you?' Richard offered solicitously once he had parked outside her apartment building.

She swallowed hard, shaking her head. 'I'm really sorry about this, Richard, but I—I think it would be best if I just went straight to bed.' And buried her head under the covers until this nightmare went away!

'I'll call you tomorrow,' Richard called after her, obviously still dazed by the abrupt end to their evening.

Harrie didn't answer him, hurrying up to her apartment as if a pack of wolves were at her heels. Or just one wolf, she realised sickly once she had reached her apartment and locked her door behind her.

Had she been wrong in her defence of Richard to her father and Quinn? Or had she just imagined the look on

Richard's face as he'd watched Corinne and David leave the restaurant, as if he were studying specimens under a microscope?

She had been so adamant, so sure in her defence of Richard—what was she going to do if her father and Quinn had been right about him all along?

If that turned out to be the case—and she so hoped that it wouldn't!—one thing she did know for certain; she would never give Quinn McBride the satisfaction of knowing how stupid she had been.

But, with any luck, she would never see him again, anyway!

CHAPTER FIVE

NERVOUS.

He was nervous, damn it. And it wasn't an emotion Quinn was either familiar or comfortable with!

He should be angry with Harrie for being the cause of his uncertainty, at the unaccustomed way his heart was pounding in his chest as he waited the long, interminable minutes it was taking for her to answer his ring of the security bell to her apartment. But somehow anger was the last thing he felt...!

With any luck, in a few minutes, he was going to see Harrie again. And the forty-eight hours since he'd last seen her somehow seemed much longer than that. No doubt she would be spitting fire and brimstone at him again, but he probably wouldn't recognise her if she were any other way. In fact, he grinned just at the thought of seeing those flashing green eyes again!

'Yes?' her tense response finally came over the intercom.

Some of Quinn's nervousness abated; at least she was at home! 'I told you I would visit you in your sickbed,' he drawled mockingly, instantly rewarded by what he guessed to be a stunned silence on the other end of the intercom.

She had recognised his reference, if not his voice, and she wasn't pleased to know he was her caller! Not that he had expected a warm welcome, he acknowledged ruefully. Harrie was not a woman who shielded her real emotions behind a polite façade. Thank goodness.

'Sorry to disappoint you, Quinn,' she finally snapped back, 'but I'm not in my sickbed!'

'And I'm not disappointed,' he returned dryly. 'Can I come up?'

'No,' came her instant response.

Quinn grinned again. 'That isn't very polite, Harrie,' he chided mockingly.

'If it's politeness you want, I suggest you find someone else to talk to!' she snapped sarcastically.

He couldn't stop grinning, damn it! Even defensive and rude, Harrie made him smile. He shook his head; if she thought she was putting him off, she was mistaken!

'I would rather talk to you,' he murmured softly.

'If you've come to gloat—'

'I haven't.' He sobered, knowing exactly what she was referring to. And it didn't please him that he had hurt her. It was the last thing he wanted to do!

'I don't believe you,' Harrie told him wearily. 'And who told you where I live?' she added suspiciously.

'Guess,' he said dryly.

She gave a heavy sigh. 'I'll talk to my father later!'

'Press the button and let me come up, Harrie,' he instructed firmly. 'And then you'll be able to see for yourself that I've come in peace.'

Quinn looked down at the flowers he carried, having bought them on impulse from a vendor down the street. He grimaced slightly now. Maybe they were a little over the top—they certainly looked like some sort of peace-offering!

He looked around for somewhere to dump them, dropping them over the metal railing in front of the building. 'Fear the Greeks bearing gifts' came to mind. Not that he was Greek, and the flowers weren't exactly a gift to hide his real reason for being here, but he knew Harrie well enough by now to realise exactly how she would see them!

It seemed an age before the buzzer sounded on the door to let him know he could go in, after all. He stepped quickly inside—before she could change her mind! Harrie obviously felt no friendlier towards him now than she had on Saturday. And, as he knew only too well, with good reason!

She was nowhere to be seen when the lift deposited him straight in her penthouse apartment on the top floor, giving him chance to look around. Warmth and comfort were the two things that struck him about her choice of decor; the wooden furniture was obviously golden antique oak, the cream sofa and chairs were large and comfortable, and there were cream and yellow flowers adorning the dining-table.

A woman of discerning taste, Quinn decided—except in one particular subject. Richard Heaton! His mouth tightened just at the thought of the other man, and Quinn knew it was no longer just because of his attempts to blackmail Corinne...!

'Quinn,' Harrie greeted him tightly at that moment as she came through from what he assumed was her bedroom. 'You've called at a bad time, I'm afraid, I'm just on my way out,' she told him dismissively, fixing the clasp on the gold bracelet she wore as she walked towards him.

Quinn had realised on Saturday that she was beautiful, but with her dark hair in loose curls over her shoulders and down her back, the short emerald-coloured dress she wore clinging lovingly to the perfection of her body, her legs long and slender, three-inch heels on the matching emerald-coloured shoes she wore, Harrie looked absolutely stunning. So much so that she took Quinn's breath away!

'Quinn?' she prompted impatiently at his lack of a response.

Except he wasn't without a response, the stirrings of his

body telling him that. As it would tell Harrie if he didn't soon sit down!

'Sorry,' he grimaced ruefully. 'I was just thinking that you're right—you don't look sick enough to be in bed, either!'

Harrie frowned at him. 'I'm not sure—'

'As well as giving me your address, Rome also informed me that you didn't feel well enough to be at work today.' He quirked mocking brows at her more than healthy-looking appearance.

Resentful colour highlighted her cheeks. 'He was right—I didn't!' she finally snapped.

'In that case...you've made a miraculous recovery!' Quinn drawled derisively. 'And do stop fidgeting, Harrie; surely you have time to share a drink with me before you have to leave?' he challenged mockingly—even as he moved to fold his long length gratefully in one of the comfortable armchairs!

She looked at him coldly. 'Celebrating, Quinn?' she bit out pointedly.

'Perhaps,' he drawled easily. 'What do you think?' He quirked one dark brow at her.

Angry colour now highlighted her cheeks as she glared at him. 'I think you and my father did rather a good job today of painting your sister as whiter than white, and— I'm sorry—' she sighed, holding up an apologetic hand '—that was uncalled for.' She swallowed hard. 'Jane Freeman's article in today's newspaper, on your sister, was very warm and human,' she conceded tautly.

Rome's solution to Corinne's problem had been so very simple, so simple Quinn could have kicked himself for not thinking of it first. The public would know the truth of Corinne's marriage, and the mistake she had made afterwards, but it would be done in such a way that there was no sensationalism involved in the revelation, more a tribute to the strength and courage of the woman who was to be the wife of the probable next prime minister.

And it had worked, Quinn acknowledged with inner satisfaction. Jane Freeman had interviewed Corinne as planned on Sunday morning at ten o'clock, and the story had appeared on the women's page of Rome's newspaper this morning—and so far the response to Corinne's frankness had all been positive. Several other newspapers, and a prominent television interviewer, were now interested in following up on the story, but as a tribute to Corinne, not the character assassination Richard Heaton had hinted at. Quinn just hoped it continued to be that way...

But, in the meantime, he realised it had totally upset Richard Heaton's plans for Corinne, something the other man would not be pleased about...

Quinn nodded. 'I believe so,' he conceded guardedly. 'I don't suppose your friend Richard is too happy about it, though,' he added with satisfaction.

Harrie gave a rueful shrug. 'Why don't you ask him?' She looked down at the slender watch on her wrist. 'He should be arriving in a few minutes,' she added with satisfaction.

Quinn sat forward in the armchair, his eyes narrowed. 'Are you telling me that you're dressed—like that—to go out on a date with Richard Heaton?' he rasped with rapidly rising anger.

Harrie gave an acknowledging inclination of her head. 'We're off to a literary dinner,' she told him challengingly, that air of satisfaction having deepened at the disclosure.

Quinn's scowl deepened, too. Richard Heaton was going to arrive here in a few minutes, with the intention of taking Harrie out for the evening. The former was bad enough, the latter was totally unacceptable!

His mouth twisted contemptuously. 'Your taste in friends is appalling!'

She met his furious gaze unblinkingly. 'Fortunately, my taste in enemies is much worse!'

Him. She meant *him*, damn it. And he didn't want her to think of him as her enemy. He wanted to be something much closer to her than that!

'Harrie—'

'You mentioned a drink,' she cut in smoothly, moving gracefully to the tray of drinks on the sideboard. 'What would you like? I can offer you red or white wine, and I have most of the spirits, too.' She looked across at him with polite query.

With the knowledge that Richard Heaton was to arrive here at any minute, with the intention of whisking Harrie away for the evening, a stiff brandy wouldn't go amiss!

'I'll have whatever you're having,' he muttered grimly, totally disgusted a few minutes later when he found himself in possession of a glass of orange juice!

'I may not look sick, Quinn, or have actually taken to my bed,' Harrie drawled in amusement at the grimace of distaste on his face, 'but as it happens I do have a throat infection, and the doctor recommended I not take any alcohol with the antibiotics he prescribed!'

Orange juice! Not that he didn't like juice; it was usually his first drink of the day. But it certainly wasn't what he'd had in mind for just now!

He scowled up at Harrie as she stood beside the unlit marble fireplace. 'I'm sure he also ''recommended'' you stay away from other people until you're free of infection,' he bit out tersely, placing the untouched glass of juice down on the coffee-table.

She arched dark brows. 'Frightened you might catch something, Quinn?' she taunted.

Thinking of a way to stop her going out with Richard Heaton was more like it! But, considering the other man was due here in a matter of minutes, he was probably wasting his time.

His mouth twisted. 'I was thinking more of your date for the evening,' he rasped harshly.

She shrugged. 'I've already explained the situation to Richard—and he's prepared to take the risk.'

Quinn would just bet he was! The thought of Harrie spending the evening with Richard Heaton was driving him crazy!

'I'm sure he is,' Quinn said disgustedly. 'Harrie—' He broke off as the buzzer for the door sounded on the wall beside the lift, glaring across at the offending intercom— almost as if it were Richard Heaton himself already standing there!

Harrie made no effort to move. 'I'm sure you must have somewhere else to go, Quinn...?' she prompted tautly.

She didn't want him to meet Richard Heaton any more than he thought it prudent at this particular moment to come face to face with the other man—which was more than enough reason for Quinn not to move!

He settled more comfortably into the armchair. 'Not that I can think of, no,' he returned mildly.

Her mouth tightened with impatience. 'Quinn—'

'Harrie,' he drawled unconcernedly.

She gave an irritated sigh. 'You know you have no wish to meet Richard—'

'Don't I?' he challenged softly. 'Are you sure that isn't your own wish? Your caller seems to be becoming a little anxious,' he drawled as the buzzer sounded a second time.

Her mouth set angrily. 'Just don't cause a scene in my apartment, Quinn,' she warned him irritatedly as she marched over to speak on the security intercom.

Quinn smiled grimly to himself as he listened unashamedly to her side of the intercom conversation, her voice light and friendly, but not, he noted with satisfaction, in the least breathlessly loving. Although that, he realised with less satisfaction, might just be because Harrie was all too aware of his listening presence!

Richard Heaton. In a few minutes Quinn was going to meet the man he had come to despise over the last few weeks, a man he didn't believe good enough to be in the same room as Harrie, let alone—

Let alone, what...?

Were Harrie and the other man lovers? Quinn felt nauseous just at the thought of it. But in a few minutes he was going to know the answer to that question. He knew he would be able to tell by the way Harrie and Richard reacted to each other just how intimate their relationship was.

That realisation made him angrier than ever!

And that anger wasn't in the less lessened when the other man stepped from the lift into the apartment a minute or so later, bending to kiss Harrie lightly on the lips— before calmly handing her the bouquet of flowers Quinn had minutes ago dropped over the railing outside!

Harrie accepted Richard's kiss, and the flowers, distractedly, all too aware of Quinn seated in the room behind her.

She'd spent the most miserable day on her own yesterday, her thoughts alternating between an unwanted belief in Quinn and her father's accusations concerning Richard, and then instantly contradicting those thoughts by recalling Richard's warmth and charm when the two of them were together, sure that her companion of the last few months couldn't possibly be guilty of the things he was accused of.

And that certainly had been endorsed by Richard himself when he'd telephoned her in the afternoon to see if she was feeling any better, his concern as to her well-being obviously genuine as he'd told her not to give this evening's literary dinner another thought, just to get herself well. But Harrie had assured him she was only feeling slightly under the weather, that she was sure she would be well enough to go to the dinner with him the following evening.

It had served her right when she'd woken this morning with a raging headache, and a sore throat to go with it, but at least the call in sick she had made to her father had been completely genuine!

She hadn't even seen the newspaper until her return from the chemist after picking up her prescription, but the article on Corinne Westley had done nothing to improve the way she felt.

Although looking at Richard now, his smile warm with concern as he gazed down at her, Harrie couldn't see that he had been in the least affected by that same article.

Well, of course he wasn't, she instantly berated herself; Quinn was mistaken in his accusations towards Richard, and her father was just going along with them because Richard wasn't a man of his own choosing for his eldest daughter!

'They're beautiful, Richard, thank you.' She buried her face in the fragrant blooms he had just given her—the first flowers he'd ever given her, in fact.

'You're more than welcome,' he assured her huskily. 'But I have to say their beauty can in no way compare to yours,' he added warmly.

Harrie's smile of pleasure was arrested on her lips as she heard the strangulated sound coming from the room behind her. Quinn! And the noise he'd made sounded distinctly like a muffled laugh to her!

'I have a visitor, Richard,' she told him stiltedly—before they gave Quinn anything else to laugh at! 'He was just about to leave,' she added for Quinn's benefit. 'But come

and be introduced, anyway.' She linked her hand lightly
with his as she led the way back into the sitting-room.

Quinn had stood up since she'd left the room, his expression guarded as he looked across at the man at her
side. Given the circumstances of how Quinn had told her
he felt towards Richard, Harrie supposed she should feel
grateful for the fact that he hadn't immediately crossed the
room and punched Richard in the face!

But, of course, they were all civilised people—weren't
they…?

Lord, she hoped so!

Although the look on Quinn's face as he looked at her
hand linked with Richard's didn't augur well for that hope!

'Richard Heaton, Quinn McBride.' She made the intro-
ductions as briefly as possible. A bit like lighting the blue
touch-paper—and waiting to see if the rocket would go up
or not!

Quinn, of course, made no reaction to the identity of the
other man—why should he? He had been forewarned.

But Harrie found herself watching Richard closely to
see how he reacted to knowing who Quinn was. If he did
know. After all, she hadn't made any connection herself
between Quinn and his sister, Corinne Westley…

Richard's smile was coolly polite as he released Harrie's
hand to hold his own hand out to the other man. 'A little
late in the day to be working, isn't it, Harrie?' he remarked
lightly, obviously wondering at the other man's reasons
for being here.

Quinn barely touched the other man's hand, his aqua-
blue eyes having taken on a flinty quality. 'Actually, I'm
a friend of the family,' he bit out harshly. 'Harrie tells me
the two of you are off to a literary dinner this evening…'

Harrie was recoiling from having Quinn describe himself as a 'family friend'; he and her father might have
become friends during the last few days, but she certainly

didn't consider herself any sort of friend of Quinn McBride's!

'It's a bit of a bore, but, yes,' Richard answered the older man, dressed for the part in his black evening suit and snowy-white shirt.

'I'm sure with Harrie at your side it won't be in the least boring,' Quinn came back smoothly.

Challengingly, it seemed to Harrie. Exactly what was he trying to do now?

Richard looked blank for several seconds, and then he gave a rueful smile. 'I wasn't including Harrie in that remark, of course.' His eyes were narrowed as he looked at the older man. 'Quinn McBride...' he repeated slowly. 'Now why does that name sound familiar?'

Harrie felt herself tense. Was this going to be it, the showdown between these two men, here in her apartment? She closed her eyes as she waited for the explosion.

'I have no idea,' Quinn answered Richard dismissively before turning to Harrie. 'You're looking a little pale still,' he told her huskily. 'Are you sure you feel up to going out this evening?'

She would begin to feel a whole lot better—probably recover some of her colour, too—if he would only leave! Because she knew, the longer Quinn stayed, the more chance there was he would cease to hold on to that civilised veneer she was so depending on!

'I told you earlier, I feel perfectly well again now,' she said tautly. 'And we really mustn't keep you any longer,' she encouraged lightly, the determined look in her eyes telling him just how much she wanted him to leave.

Quinn looked for a moment as if he were about to argue the point, and then he gave a stiff inclination of his head. 'I'll give you a call tomorrow. To see how you are,' he added harshly after Harrie gave him a sharply questioning look.

'There's really no need, Quinn,' she assured him dryly. 'I'm sure I shall be fully recovered by tomorrow.'

He nodded abruptly. 'I'll call you anyway. Walk me to the lift, hmm?' he prompted harshly.

Harrie gave him a startled look. Walk him to the lift...? From anyone else that would have sounded almost lover-like—from Quinn McBride it sounded like the order Harrie was sure it actually was!

'Of course,' she agreed with cool politeness. 'Help yourself to a drink, Richard.' She indicated the tray of drinks on the sideboard.

Neither man made any effort to say a polite goodbye to the other, and the tension emanating from Quinn as Harrie walked beside him to the lift was so heavy she felt she could almost reach out and touch it. Which made her realise, for the first time, just how much control Quinn must have exerted over himself the last ten minutes not to have hit Richard for the distress he felt he'd caused his beloved sister...

She reached out and touched his arm once they stood outside the lift. 'Quinn—' She broke off with a gasp as he turned to look at her, a look of such savage anger on his face it literally took her breath away. 'Quinn...?' she choked concernedly, her hand still on his rigidly tensed arm.

He glanced coldly back into the room where Richard now had his back towards them as he poured himself a glass of red wine. 'If I had met him under any other circumstances...!' he grated softly between clenched teeth, shaking his head disgustedly. 'Nice flowers,' he added scathingly.

The last few minutes had been filled with such tension she hadn't even realised she still held Richard's flowers in her hand, glancing down at them now as if she were seeing them for the first time. 'Very,' she confirmed stiltedly, frowning at the unexpectedness of the remark.

Quinn's mouth twisted derisively. 'Almost as lovely as when I purchased them half an hour ago!'

When *he*—! What—? How—? Why—?

Her thoughts were going round and round like a scratched record, damn it, Harrie realised crossly. What did Quinn mean, *he* had purchased the flowers...? And if he had, how had it ended up with Richard giving them to her?

'Remember the adage about Greeks and gifts, Harrie?' Quinn warned scornfully even as his fingers dug into her arms as he suddenly reached out to grasp hold of her. 'Especially when they happen to be someone else's gifts!' he drawled with a disgusted look in Richard's direction.

She swallowed hard. 'I don't understand—'

'Oh, I think you understand very well, Harrie,' Quinn murmured softly, his eyes hard aqua-blue as he once again glanced across at the younger man. 'It's only your stubborn pride that is making you hold on to an illusion.'

Her own eyes glittered with anger at his daring to tell her what she did or didn't understand. 'Is this the part in the conversation where you remind me of another old adage? That of pride coming before a fall?' she pointed out disgustedly at his enquiring look.

Quinn's mouth twisted mockingly. 'Oh, you're nowhere near falling yet, Harrie,' he assured her tauntingly. 'And even if you were, I would be there to pick you up,' he added grimly.

She blinked up at him, looking away as she found herself unable to meet the intensity of his gaze. 'I have no idea what you're talking about,' she muttered hardly—not sure that she wanted to know, either!

Quinn released her as abruptly as he'd reached out to

hold her. 'Get rid of him, Harrie,' he warned harshly. 'Before I do it for you,' he added with grim determination.

Harrie gasped at his arrogance. But before she could think of a suitable reply, he had stepped into the waiting lift and pressed the button for the ground floor, the doors closing quietly before it—and Quinn!—began their descent.

Now that he had actually gone, Harrie couldn't seem to move. What had Quinn meant about the flowers? If he had bought them for her, then why hadn't he given them to her? And how was it they'd come to be in Richard's possession?

But more to the point, what had he mean by that last remark...?

'Harrie...?'

She turned to find Richard lounging against the wall as he watched her intently. Forcing those questions to the back of her mind, she gave him a bright, meaningless smile. 'Sorry.' She grimaced. 'Quinn can be a little—overpowering,' she understated.

Quinn wasn't just overpowering—he was all-consuming! And, she acknowledged with a troubled frown as she looked at Richard, Quinn made the younger man fade into insignificance by comparison.

What was happening to her? Quinn McBride wasn't actually getting to her, was he? Surely not—he was even more unsuitable for her than he claimed Richard to be!

'So I believe,' Richard answered her remark, straightening away from the wall, his eyes narrowed as he looked across at her. 'And now that he's gone, perhaps you would like to tell me just what the hell is going on,' he added in a silkily soft voice.

'With Quinn?' She gave a lightly dismissing laugh as she walked over to join Richard. 'Why, nothing—'

'No, not just ''with Quinn'',' Richard cut in gratingly,

his face distorted with anger now. 'Until a short time ago I believed that what happened today was just bad luck as far as I was concerned, a case of bad timing on Jane's part, or, at worst, a lack of communication between colleagues. But then I arrive here and find you cosily ensconced with none other than Quinn McBride. So I'll ask you again, Harrie,' he bit out harshly. 'What the hell is going on?'

Harrie looked at him wordlessly, shaken by the sudden change that had come over him. He was no more the charmingly attentive man she was used to, but one consumed by fiercely burning anger.

Jane. He had mentioned a colleague called Jane. Jane Freeman...? The woman who had written today's article on Corinne Westley...

My God, Harrie realised as she looked at Richard dazedly; *he* had also known exactly who *Quinn* was all along...!

CHAPTER SIX

IT TOOK all of the couple of minutes that passed as the lift made its descent to the ground floor for Quinn to realise there was no way he could just calmly walk away.

For one thing, he detested the idea of leaving Harrie alone with Richard Heaton. And for another, the man may have seemed charmingly vague when Quinn had been introduced to him, but surely a man with Richard Heaton's hard-hitting reputation, especially where his work was concerned, would have made himself aware of all of Corinne Westley's background, but especially the fact that the only family she had was an older brother—and *his* name was Quinn McBride!

The man had been putting on an act!

The more Quinn thought about it, the more sure he became, pressing the button for the recall of the lift, stepping agitatedly inside once the doors had opened, his movements restless as he waited for the lift to reach the penthouse floor.

At which time the doors didn't open!

And wouldn't be opened, Quinn realised frustratedly, until Harrie released the security button inside her apartment!

Trust Harrie, Quinn muttered to himself agitatedly, to live in an apartment that kept the 'bad guy' in and the 'good guy' out!

Then he realised he was being unfair to her. And probably making an idiot of himself too. What real reason did he have, apart from his own aversion to Richard Heaton, for coming back up to Harrie's apartment? And exactly what was he going to say when and if he did get back inside her apartment: 'unhand that woman'? It sounded like something out of a Victorian novel, and a cheap one at that!

Better to just go back downstairs, return home, and do as he had said he would—telephone Harrie in the morning. Early. Very early.

Harrie!

He could hear Harrie's voice from inside the apartment now, slightly raised, Richard Heaton's reply a soft murmur, inaudibly so. Either the two of them were nearing the door as they prepared to leave for their dinner—or they were arguing!

Quinn knew which he hoped it was, although if it were the latter, with his own recent departure, the probability was the argument was about him—or Corinne...!

He banged loudly on the lift door. 'Harrie? Harrie! Open the door, damn it,' he swore as impatience took over from prudence.

So he made a fool of himself—so what? He had a feeling he was going to do that some time in the future over Harrie Summer, anyway, so why not make a start now?

'Harrie, I said—' He broke off abruptly as the lift doors swooshed open, a dishevelled Harrie standing on the other side of them, her beautiful dark hair tousled and untidy, her scarlet-coloured lip-gloss ever so slightly smudged on puffy lips.

Quinn's heart sank at the sight of her. He had seen her looking this wantonly beautiful only once before. When *he* had kissed her. And the thought of having interrupted Richard Heaton doing the same thing made him feel—

'Quinn!' Harrie cried thankfully, grabbing hold of his arm and pulling him into the apartment. 'Richard was just leaving. Weren't you?' she added pointedly, her hand tucked snugly into the crook of Quinn's arm as she glared angrily across at Richard Heaton—murderously! Because if Harrie had been kissed in the last few minutes it certainly wasn't something she had enjoyed!

Richard Heaton had adopted a slightly scornful pose as he looked across at them unconcernedly. 'Was I?' he sneered. 'I thought we were going out,' he reminded Harrie dryly.

'Then you thought wrong!' Her eyes flashed deeply emerald. 'I would prefer it if you just left,' she added tautly, her hand gripping Quinn's arm so tightly now her nails were digging into his flesh through the material of his jacket.

Exactly what had transpired in the few minutes since his departure, Quinn wondered savagely, to have created this total aversion to the other man inside Harrie? As if, Quinn decided after another glance at her dishevelled appearance, he really needed to ask himself that!

'You heard her, Heaton,' Quinn rasped, squeezing Harrie's hand reassuringly before releasing himself from her grasp and walking over to stand mere inches away from the other man. 'And I would advise you to make it sooner rather than later.' His voice was dangerously soft now.

Richard Heaton gave an unabashed shrug. 'Oh, don't worry, I'll leave peacefully,' he drawled mockingly, a humourless smile curving his lips. 'But this isn't over yet,' he added assuredly. 'The first round may have gone to you, but it certainly wasn't a knockout!'

The gloves were most assuredly off, Quinn acknowledged grimly. 'It isn't just me you've—offended, Heaton,' he told the other man contemptuously. 'And I can assure you that it's a mistake—on your part—to have made an adversary of Rome Summer, too,' he added warningly.

Blond brows were raised over mocking blue eyes. 'I was just doing my job—'

'I don't think any of us see it that way,' Quinn ground out savagely.

Richard Heaton shrugged. 'Perhaps we'll just let the general public decide that, hmm?'

Quinn's mouth tightened. 'I think that, after this evening, you may just find yourself without a newspaper to print anything you have to say!' His eyes glittered threateningly.

'Fortunately, Rome Summer doesn't own all the newspapers,' the other man scored.

'Maybe he doesn't,' Quinn conceded shortly. 'But no reputable newspaper would touch anything you want to write about Corinne after the publication of today's article about her!' But unfortunately, as Quinn was sure Heaton knew only too well, one of the more lurid tabloids probably would! 'So unless you want to find yourself completely out in the cold in the newspaper world, I would advise you to proceed with extreme caution,' he added warmly.

'Now who's issuing threats?' Richard Heaton taunted, but less confidently, Quinn thought.

Or, rather, hoped! Corinne had looked so much better when Quinn had left the house earlier this evening, happier and more confident than Quinn had seen her look for a very long time. Of course David's love and support, on being told of Corinne's unhappy love affair after the death of her husband, had gone a long way to achieving that effect, but Quinn knew it was also due to the fact that his sister believed the nightmare of being blackmailed was over. But, as Quinn was all too aware, Richard Heaton still had the means to shatter that fragile happiness if he should choose to do so...!

Nevertheless, Quinn's smile was completely confident. 'I think I should warn you—' his voice was silkily soft

'—you will find me a much more formidable adversary than Corinne could ever have been!'

'No doubt.' The younger man gave an acknowledging inclination of his head. 'Just how close a "friend" of the Summer family are you?' he added speculatively after an insulting glance at the silent Harrie.

Quinn's mouth tightened into a thin line. 'Very,' he bit out tautly.

Richard Heaton gave a scathing laugh. 'That's what I thought,' he murmured, walking past Quinn to stop in front of Harrie.

To give Harrie her due, Quinn noted with admiration, she met the other man's scornful gaze unflinchingly. In that moment she had the look of a sleek black jaguar, green eyes blazing with challenge. And Quinn knew that to him she'd never looked more beautiful!

'No hard feelings, Harrie?' Richard Heaton prompted softly.

For a brief moment she looked nonplussed by the comment, and then her expression turned to disgust. 'As I don't intend even so much as thinking of you again—the answer to that is a definite no!' she bit out forcefully.

The other man laughed softly. 'It's a pity you feel that way, Harrie,' Richard drawled. 'Because, after all that we've shared together these last few months—I'm going to find great difficulty in forgetting you!'

Quinn felt the fury rising within him as he took in the full implication of the other man's words. Richard Heaton and Harrie *had* been lovers, after all...!

Something very like a physical pain ripped through his chest, to be quickly quelled again. Harrie was twenty-nine years old, for goodness' sake, and not an inexperienced child. He wouldn't want her himself if she were!

But, nevertheless, the thought of her and Richard Heaton

together, intimately entwined in each other's arms, made him feel ill...

'Get out, Richard,' Harrie told him dully. 'And take your flowers with you!' She picked the blooms up from the side-table where she had placed them earlier, thrusting them towards him.

Richard Heaton made no effort to take them from her. 'Keep them.' He pressed the lift button. 'As a reminder of me!' he added tauntingly.

'How can they be—when it appears you didn't even buy them for me?' Harrie spat the words at him.

Richard Heaton gave Quinn a speculative look before stepping inside the waiting lift and closing the doors behind him.

Silence followed the other man's departure. Harrie seemed unable to move away from her position near the lift, and Quinn's head was still full of visions of Harrie in the other man's arms. And worse! The more he tried to push those visions from his mind, the more determined they seemed to be to want to stay, vividly graphic—and achingly painful!

At last Harrie's breath released in a shaky sigh as she turned slowly to face Quinn. And she knew the disgust she could see in his expression wasn't all directed at Richard!

Well, Quinn couldn't possibly feel any more disgusted with her than she did with herself! She had been so wrong about Richard, the full extent of his deception becoming apparent after Quinn's departure; the insults he'd levelled at her, as the spoilt, gullible daughter of Rome Summer, had been only the beginning!

She swallowed down the nausea as she thought of the way Richard had pulled her roughly into his arms and tried to force her to— The bruises she was sure she would have on her arms by morning were as nothing compared to the ones in her heart!

Quinn and her father had been right about Richard's duplicity all the time!

She closed her eyes as she remembered the hurtful words Richard had so deliberately thrown at her. He was angry at losing his hold over Corinne Westley, she knew, furious at the way he'd been duped by her father and Quinn—but that didn't take the sting out of the string of insults he had launched at her.

Whoever had quoted that adage about 'sticks and stones may break my bones, but words can never hurt me', had been so wrong; the bruises to her flesh would heal within a day or two, whereas the personal insults Richard had verbally lashed her with would never be forgotten...

She let out a shaky sigh. 'So you were right after all,' she said dully.

Quinn scowled. 'I can assure you, it gives me no pleasure to have been so,' he rasped harshly.

Harrie swallowed hard, not altogether sure she believed him. 'If you will excuse me—I'll just get rid of these!' She held up the much detested flowers, no longer caring which man they came from; they were a reminder of this evening, and they were going in the bin—where they belonged!

She staggered once in the privacy of her kitchen, leaning against one of the work units, her legs feeling weak and shaky. Richard was everything—and more!—that her father and Quinn had claimed him to be. And, after her fierce defence of him, she didn't know what to do next.

That she would have to go out of here and face Quinn again she knew for certain; there was no way he would just quietly leave and give her time to lick her wounds. If only she didn't feel so stupid!

Well, she *was* stupid, she muttered with self-recrimination, her despair starting to be replaced by anger. Stupid, and arrogant, in believing that she knew best where Richard was concerned.

But, stupid or not, that did not mean she was going to give Quinn the satisfaction of seeing just how shaken she was by all of this...

She thrust the flowers in the bin before turning and walking determinedly back out to the sitting-room. 'I think a glass of wine is called for, don't you?' she announced brightly, knowing an inner pleasure when Quinn turned from the bookcase he had been looking through, dark brows raised in surprise at her cheerful tone.

Well—like Richard—she might be 'down', but she wasn't 'out'!

'Red or white?' she offered lightly.

'White—thank you,' Quinn accepted slowly, his lids narrowed as he watched her warily.

If he was expecting her to collapse in an emotional heap, he was in for a disappointment, Harrie determined firmly. She would wait until Quinn had left before she did that!

The half-full glass of red wine that stood near the drinks tray was a sharp reminder of Richard's abrupt departure minutes earlier. Harrie carefully avoiding so much as looking at it as she poured the two glasses of wine from the cooled bottle of Chablis.

'Here we are.' She handed Quinn one of the glasses of wine before taking a grateful sip from her own glass. Not exactly nectar, but it was welcome nonetheless!

Quinn made no attempt to drink his own wine. 'What are we drinking to?' he prompted hardly.

'Absent friends?' Harrie returned sharply.

Quinn drew in a harsh breath. 'Harrie—'

'Or perhaps you would like to make a toast to your sister?' she cut in tautly over his protest. 'I'm sure she must be feeling relieved that all of this is over.' Whereas Harrie felt that, for her, it was only just beginning!

How on earth was she going to face her father again after the things she had said to him during her defence of Richard?

The same way she was facing Quinn again, she told herself firmly; with a mask of indifference very firmly over her inner emotions!

'But is it?' Quinn came back softly. 'Over, I mean,' he explained at Harrie's frowning look.

'But of course it is,' she scorned, moving away to stand over near the window that looked down over the beauty that was London on an early summer's evening. 'Richard was just blustering at the end,' she dismissed with distaste. 'I'm sure your remark about the possibility of finding himself unemployable, if he continued with this, hit home.' If it hadn't, then Richard was more of a fool than she had given him credit for—because her father was not an adversary who pulled his punches!

'Maybe.' Quinn shrugged. 'And how about you? How do you feel about him now?' he clarified as Harrie gave him a blank look.

Did this man have no tact, no sense of where he could and couldn't venture? Obviously not, she decided irritably as Quinn continued to look at her questioningly.

She drew in a deep breath. 'I've obviously—seen another side of Richard this evening,' she began guardedly. 'I can't say it's a side I particularly care for.'

'And?' Quinn prompted harshly.

Harrie frowned. 'And what?'

His glass landed with a loud crash on the coffee-table. 'Will you be seeing Heaton again, damn it?' he bit out savagely.

She blinked at his vehemence. 'I'm sure you heard me tell him I wouldn't be,' she answered dazedly.

Quinn's mouth twisted. 'You've said the same to me, several times—and here I still am!'

Ah. 'It's hardly the same thing, is it, Quinn?' she dismissed hardly. 'You aren't here by invitation,' she added pointedly.

Those aqua-blue eyes became as stormy as a wind-tossed sea. 'Forgive me if I'm wrong,' he bit out coldly, 'but I could have sworn you invited me in—actually, dragged me in is probably a better description!—the second time I arrived this evening!'

Harrie drew in a sharp breath at his deliberate cruelty. 'You're enjoying this, aren't you, Quinn?' she scorned. 'You—' The rest of her words were cut off as Quinn's mouth came down possessively on hers!

Not again! It was just too much. It had been bad enough that Richard believed he could treat her exactly how he pleased now that he had no further need to hide behind that charming façade—because façade it most certainly had been; Harrie had seen a completely different side to him as he'd forced his kisses and caresses on her.

But there was no way she was going to take the same insulting behavior from Quinn McBride. Especially when he claimed to have saved her from the other man's unwanted attentions!

But as savagely as the kiss had begun, it now gentled to questing passion, Quinn's mouth moving searchingly over hers, sipping and tasting, his tongue running over the sensitivity of her inner lips.

Harrie could feel herself melting in a way she'd never known before. There was not a thought in her head now other than the sensation of Quinn's possession of her mouth, clinging to the broad width of his shoulders as one of his hands sought and found the pointed tip of her breast, the nipple instantly responding to the warm caress.

Heated desire coursed through her body like molten

flame, her legs becoming entwined with his as she could
feel the pulsing hardness of his own arousal.

His lips left hers to trail a path down to the pointed
hunger of her breast, her fingers becoming entwined in the
thick darkness of the hair at his nape as she held him closer
to her, wanting, needing, so much more!

She desperately wanted Quinn to make love to her!

Even as she acknowledged that aching need she
wrenched her mouth away from his, stunned at her own
admission. 'No, Quinn!' she gasped, breathing hard as she
pushed ineffectually against the hardness of his chest.
Ineffectually, because Quinn was much stronger than her,
and he didn't want to release her.

He looked down at her with those stormy aqua-coloured
eyes. 'No?' he grated.

'No!' She shook her head firmly, looking up at him
pleadingly. 'Quinn, we can't do this!' She grimaced pro-
testingly, giving up all effort of trying to release herself,
knowing she was just wasting her energy. And from the
purposeful look in Quinn's eyes, she might still have need
of that!

'Can't we?' he grated. 'Strange, I thought we already
were.'

'Not like this, Quinn,' she groaned. 'You'll only regret
it,' she added warningly—knowing that if he wouldn't, she
certainly would!

'Why?' he scorned. 'Because you'll set your father on
me?' he taunted.

Colour warmed her cheeks as he misunderstood her
words of caution for a threat. 'I can fight my own battles,
thank you!'

'Then could it be because you'll hate me "afterwards"?' He gave a derisive snort at his own suggestion.
'You've already made it more than clear that's how you

feel about me, so what have I got to lose?' he added dismissively.

Harrie swallowed hard. 'I don't hate you, Quinn—'

'Dislike me, then,' he cut in scathingly. 'What's the difference?' He shrugged scornfully.

'I don't dislike you, either,' she said huskily.

She had thought she did dislike Quinn. For his arrogance in his initial assumption that she was the mistress of Rome Summer. For his scorn and derision towards the man she had thought she loved. Thought—because she no longer felt anything but loathing towards Richard! But just now, when Quinn had thought—correctly!—that Richard would turn on her once the two of them were alone, Quinn had come back to see if she'd needed any help. There was no way she could hate or dislike the man who had done that...

Or deny that seconds ago she'd been as desperate for him to make love to her as he appeared to want to do so!

Good grief—did that mean she actually *liked* Quinn McBride?

Ridiculous!

She was grateful to him, that was all, and that gratitude had raged completely out of control.

Quinn was looking down at her uncertainly, obviously trying to read her thoughts from her expression. Well, there was no way she was going to allow him to read those particular thoughts!

Especially as she hadn't had the time herself to sit down and think them through logically!

'Let me go, Quinn,' she requested again quietly. 'Let's drink our wine and—'

'And then I can leave!' he finished derisively, releasing her as abruptly as he had taken her into his arms, turning away disgustedly.

Harrie sighed, feeling suddenly cold without the protective warmth of his arms. And unsure whether that disgust was directed at her or at himself! 'This has not been a particularly—pleasant evening for me, Quinn—'

'And I've done nothing to improve it,' he acknowledged harshly, turning to pick up his previously untouched glass of wine, throwing the contents to the back of his throat. 'You're right, Harrie, this is not a good idea,' he rasped harshly. 'I'll leave you to—well, to enjoy the rest of your evening—'

'That's hardly likely!' she put in self-derisively.

'Unmolested,' he finished grimly, turning away to walk stiffly towards the lift.

'Quinn...?' Harrie called after him uncertainly.

He glanced back briefly. 'Yes?' he prompted coldly.

She moistened dry lips before replying, not quite able to meet his gaze. 'I would like to thank you—'

'Thank me?' he repeated incredulously.

She nodded, shuddering slightly. 'If you hadn't come back, when you did—'

'You would have handled the situation, Harrie,' he assured her firmly. 'After all,' he added tauntingly, 'you *are* Rome Summer's eldest daughter!'

She couldn't help smiling at his attempt at mocking himself for his initial assumptions concerning herself and Rome. 'So I am,' she acknowledged huskily.

Quinn gave a brief nod. 'Don't let anything Richard Heaton said or did get to you, Harrie,' he advised harshly. 'You are Rome's daughter, but you're also yourself. And Harrie Summer is a pretty formidable person in her own right—as I know to my cost!' he added self-derisively.

Harrie watched him leave, standing unmoving as he stepped into the lift, the doors closing behind him, the light overhead telling of the lift's descent to the ground floor.

Quinn had gone, Harrie acknowledged dully...

And now that he had she wished he were still here.

If only to save her from her own thoughts, she acknowledged shakily. Because, as she already knew only too well, they weren't all going to be recriminations against Richard!

Because if she hadn't called a halt to the situation when she did, Quinn would still be here now, and the two of them would be making love...

And Quinn McBride was an enigma to her. So cool and detached that first day, so scornful of what he thought she was, even more so once he realised it was Richard she was involved with and not Rome.

But Quinn had been anything but cool this evening, either before or after Richard's arrival. Her skin still burned from his kisses and caresses, her breasts, swollen and aroused, aching with that unfulfilled need.

How could that be? she asked herself self-recriminatingly. Until a few hours ago she'd believed herself in love with Richard. Now just the thought of ever seeing him again made her feel ill.

Whereas the thought of never seeing Quinn again—more than just a possibility—made her feel just as ill...!

What on earth was wrong with her?

But was there actually anything wrong with her? Wasn't it perfectly natural that she would have strong feelings towards the person who had, effectively, just saved her from another man's forced attentions?

Then why, she asked herself seconds later, after dropping down weakly into one of her armchairs, were there hot tears falling down her cheeks? And not because of Richard's betrayal, but because Quinn had gone, and she didn't know when or if she would ever see him again...?

CHAPTER SEVEN

'SO TELL me, Quinn,' Rome drawled, a teasing glint in his eyes as he lounged across from Quinn in a chair in the sitting-room of his estate home, 'just how much longer did you think you could stay away from my daughter?'

He had tried, Quinn groaned inwardly, really tried, to keep out of Harrie's way, to give her time to lick the wounds Richard Heaton's betrayal had undoubtedly left her with. But in the end a week had been as long as he could stand, Quinn acknowledged.

'You invited me here for the weekend,' Quinn reminded the other man dryly—although he was aware, as Rome was, that the invitation had been at his own instigation.

He had telephoned the older man on Friday afternoon, with the excuse that the two of them needed to discuss the events—or, rather, non-events!—of the week, knowing from past experience that the other man wouldn't have had any free time that afternoon in which they could have had a general chat. Rome's invitation for Quinn to spend the weekend at the Summer estate had been exactly what Quinn had been hoping for; at least here he stood some chance of accidentally bumping into Harrie!

Rome quirked blond brows. 'Would you rather I hadn't?' he teased.

That all depended...on whether or not Harrie intended coming down here this weekend too!

Quinn shrugged. 'The Richard Heaton situation seems to have gone very quiet.' He deliberately misunderstood the other man.

'On both fronts, so I understand,' Rome acknowledged

dryly. 'Don't pretend to look so mystified, Quinn; Harrie has told me what took place on Monday evening,' he added grimly.

Not all of it, Quinn would wager! He still had difficulty himself in coming to terms with the way his own emotions had raged out of control once Richard Heaton had left Harrie's apartment on Monday evening, let alone that briefly—too briefly!—Harrie had responded as heatedly. There was no way Harrie would have told her father about that!

Although, from Rome's earlier comment, he seemed to realise *something* had happened between Quinn and Harrie...

'Then you know that Richard Heaton has finally shown Harrie his real self, too,' Quinn said harshly, remembering exactly in what way he had shown that side of himself to Harrie.

'Mmm,' Rome acknowledged abruptly. 'And, believe me, it wasn't easy for Harrie to admit to me,' he added grimly.

Quinn could imagine that all too easily; Harrie's pride had been damaged on Monday as much as anything else. It was to her credit that she had swallowed that pride and admitted her mistake to her father...

'Needless to say,' Rome rasped harshly, 'Heaton no longer works for my newspaper.'

Or anyone else yet, if Quinn's information was correct. And he had no reason to believe it wasn't. But, surely, there lay the danger; at the moment they had no idea what the other man was doing...

'I've heard on good authority that Heaton has decided to look for employment in the States.' Rome seemed to read some of his thoughts. 'I have it on even better authority,' he continued, 'that he's going to be successful!'

Quinn frowned across at Rome. How could he possibly know—?

'I have business interests in several publications over there, Quinn,' Rome told him ruefully. 'And, believe me, Heaton's employment contract is going to be bound up so tight he won't be able to sneeze without asking permission first!' he added grimly.

Quinn looked at the older man admiringly. But, then, he had known there had to be a harder side to Rome than he'd previously seen; the man couldn't have been as successful in business as he was if there hadn't been.

'Don't worry, Quinn, Heaton is well taken care of,' Rome said assuredly. 'And your sister looked extremely happy in the photographs I saw of her in the newspapers this last week,' he added with satisfaction.

'She is,' Quinn confirmed.

Now that the threat to her happiness with David had been removed, Corinne had ceased to look worried and drawn, throwing herself into her role as David's partner with new vigour and enjoyment, and their wedding plans were moving along briskly too.

'So how about answering my earlier question?' Rome prompted teasingly. 'Harrie,' he reminded as Quinn gave him a blank look.

Quinn had known exactly which question the other man had meant—he simply wasn't sure how to answer it. Because he wasn't sure of anything where Harrie was concerned, let alone how he felt about seeing her again!

Part of him very badly wanted to see her again, but the other side of him, that cautious, detached side of him, questioned what he was going to do with her when he did see her. That he wanted her, he didn't doubt, but actually becoming involved in an affair with her was something else entirely.

Harrie was nothing like the women he usually became

involved with. She certainly didn't give off any clear signals that a brief, uncomplicated affair was what she wanted. Besides, Quinn had never known—and liked—the father of any of the other women he'd been involved with, either!

This desire he had for Harrie was a complication he hadn't really had time to work out yet...

Just walking away and never seeing Harrie again was unacceptable to him, but the alternative—! Even if Harrie were willing, he did not want to get seriously involved with her—with any woman!

One thing he was very sure of: marriage—to any woman—did not figure in his immediate plans.

Quinn gave a dismissive shrug. 'I don't know what you want, or expect, me to say to that, Rome. Of course I'm concerned about Harrie; she was very upset on Monday evening.' He frowned grimly at the memory.

'Only concerned?' Rome taunted, blue eyes gleaming speculatively. 'You know, Quinn,' he continued softly, 'you're going to have enough of a battle on your hands convincing Harrie into a relationship—without fighting your own feelings too!'

Quinn sat up defensively in his armchair, his expression guarded as he looked across at the older man. 'I think you've misconstrued the situation, Rome,' he began coldly.

'I don't think so,' the other man drawled confidently. 'Remind me to tell you some time of the battle I had trying to woo the girls' mother,' he murmured fondly. 'Harrie is very like her,' he added pointedly. 'And not just in looks.'

'I—'

'Believe me, Quinn,' Rome continued firmly. 'The ones you have to fight for are the ones worth having!'

Quinn felt as if he were becoming more and more entangled in a web he was going to have trouble getting out of. Maybe it would be better if he left now.

He turned sharply towards the door as someone entered after the briefest of knocks, breathing a sigh of relief when he saw it was Audrey Archer, Rome's personal assistant. As long as it wasn't Harrie!

Idiot! he instantly chided himself. As Rome had already guessed, it was Harrie that Quinn had come here to see...!

Audrey Archer gave him a polite smile before turning to her employer. 'You asked me to let you know as soon as we heard from Andie,' she reminded economically. 'She rang through on her mobile a few minutes ago. She and Harrie will be here in about fifteen minutes.' Having delivered her message, Audrey didn't linger in the room, obviously busy with other things.

Not only Harrie, but the youngest Summer sister too, Quinn realised with an inward groan. Hell!

He stood up abruptly. 'I think I had better be on my way—'

'You were invited for the weekend, Quinn,' Rome reminded softly.

He nodded. 'I don't want to interrupt what looks like being a family time—'

'You won't be,' Rome instantly assured him. 'I have several other guests arriving later this afternoon.'

Cornered. And it was his own doing, Quinn acknowledged self-disgustedly. But would it really be so bad? He had wanted to see Harrie again, and it looked as if he was very shortly going to do that. And if there were other guests, then his being here wouldn't look too contrived. Would it...?

Oh, damn it; he wanted to see Harrie again, to look at her, to just drink her in. And if he had to do that surrounded by a lot of other people, it was probably for the best. Perhaps he wouldn't make such an idiot of himself then!

Although Rome's interest in his attraction to Harrie was a little unnerving...

A matchmaking father in the background hadn't entered into his thoughts about Harrie, let alone any relationship he'd had in mind.

A note for future reference, Quinn, he told himself ruefully; never get even close to the woman's father, let alone make a friend out of him!

Although all of those thoughts went out of his head fifteen minutes later when he heard the arrival of a car outside on the driveway, remembering all too vividly how Harrie had looked the last time he had seen her, her dark hair tousled, her lips swollen from the passionate kisses they had just shared, those green eyes mistily sleepy in her arousal.

And how much he had longed, in the last five days, to see her looking like that again!

But the look of intense dislike that washed over her face, when she entered the room a few minutes later and saw him sitting there with her father, did not give him too much hope of that happening in the near future. If ever!

Her father and Quinn McBride!

And sitting here so cosily together, as if the two of them had known each other years, instead of just the week that Harrie actually knew it to be.

What could the two of them be plotting together now? was her next thought as she studied the two of them with narrowed eyes. Someone's downfall, she didn't doubt.

'Rome,' she greeted abruptly, bending to give him a perfunctory kiss on the cheek, still vaguely resentful of the part he'd played in Richard's downfall. Oh, she accepted that Richard had been everything her father and Quinn had claimed him to be, but that didn't mean her own pride hadn't suffered as a result of it. 'Quinn.' She straightened to greet him tensely, her eyes narrowed with suspicion now.

Quinn stood up, and for a moment—a brief, panicked moment!—Harrie thought he was going to step forward and greet her as familiarly as she had her father.

But he merely gave an abrupt inclination of his head. 'Harrie,' he rasped as economically.

She turned back to her father. 'Andie still seems to be suffering from that flu she had last weekend; she's gone to lie down for a while before dinner.'

Rome scowled at this news. 'Damn it, this has gone on long enough; I've a good mind to get a doctor in to her.'

Harrie smiled, shaking her head. 'You know how Andie feels about doctors.'

'She's twenty-five now, not five!' their father rasped impatiently as he stood up.

Her sister Andie had acquired a dislike of doctors, and hospitals, since the age of five, when she'd had to have her tonsils removed. It had become something of a family joke as, over the years, Andie had flatly refused to consult a doctor over anything, preferring to just take to her bed until she felt better.

Not that Harrie felt disposed into explaining that to the obviously puzzled Quinn! Nothing about her family was any of this man's business.

'You can try telling her that, if you like.' Harrie shrugged at her father. 'But I doubt she will listen,' she added from experience. The mildest tempered of the three sisters, Andie could nevertheless become a spitting virago if pushed into a corner. And Harrie didn't doubt that Andie would put suggesting calling in a doctor under that heading.

'I'm going to try anyway,' Rome said grimly, heading towards the door.

Great, Harrie muttered crossly; within two minutes of her arrival she was left alone with Quinn McBride. The last person she wanted to be alone with. Ever.

It hadn't been the easiest of weeks, having to come to terms with Richard's duplicity, her response to Quinn's kisses and caresses, and then finally having to admit to her father that he'd been right about Richard all along.

Although, of the three, she knew which had been the hardest to live with!

And being alone with the cause of this major discomfort was not what she wanted right now.

'How is your sister?' she enquired politely, her gaze not quite making contact with Quinn's as he stood across the room.

'Very well. Thank you for asking,' he added abruptly.

Very polite, weren't they? Harrie thought. But, then, in the circumstances, what else could they be...?

Her father hadn't mentioned that Quinn McBride would be here too this weekend. Deliberately so? Probably, she inwardly acknowledged. Her father was a grand manipulator—and he had known damn well she wouldn't have come within fifty miles of the estate if she'd known Quinn was here!

Every time she thought of that time in Quinn's arms, of the intimacies they'd shared, she cringed with embarrassment. And God knew what Quinn thought of her behaviour!

'No Danie this weekend?'

Harrie looked across at him blankly for several seconds, and then his question penetrated her tortured thoughts. 'She'll be along later,' she answered lightly. 'My father has several other weekend guests arriving this afternoon.'

It was just a pity he hadn't told her that Quinn was to be amongst their number.

His mouth twisted ruefully. 'So he's just informed me.'

'There will be even more arriving for champagne brunch tomorrow.' She grimaced—the 'surprise' her father had presented *her* with took on more the form of a nightmare.

On Monday night she had initially been devastated at the thought of never seeing Quinn again, but as the days had passed she'd been grateful for the fact; how could she ever face him again after her wanton behaviour!

Well, she was facing Quinn now—and it was just as awkward and uncomfortable as she had known it would be!

'Don't be too hard on your father,' Quinn drawled now. 'He only invited me here late yesterday afternoon,' he explained at Harrie's frowning look.

Still time enough for her father to have warned her. If he'd wanted to. Which he obviously hadn't.

'Harrie—'

'Quinn—'

They both began talking at once, only to break off as abruptly, looking at each other warily now.

'You first,' Quinn invited ruefully.

She twisted her hands together in front of her. 'I just wanted to say that—' she drew in a ragged breath, still unable to look at him directly '—Monday evening. What happened.' She could feel the hot colour entering her cheeks as she spoke of that embarrassing incident. 'I was—very—emotional.' She swallowed hard. 'After what had happened with Richard. And I had drunk some wine, too, after the doctor warned me not to with the antibiotics—'

'You know, Harrie,' Quinn cut in softly, 'this way you have of meeting things head on is only one of the things I like about you.'

Now she did look at him, her heart pounding in her chest as she took in his appearance for the first time, the casual black denims and pale blue shirt adding to his ruggedness, the relaxed handsomeness of his face only making her heart beat faster.

She'd never just looked at a man before and known that she physically wanted him. But with Quinn...!

'Only one of the things?' she challenged mockingly, defensive in her feelings of weakness towards this man.

Quinn's mouth quirked with amusement. 'Fishing, Harrie?' he taunted.

'No! Certainly not,' she corrected mildly. 'If you will excuse me, Quinn,' she added abruptly, 'I think I'll just go up and check on Andie.'

'It seems to me that there are already enough people 'checking' on Andie,' he drawled derisively. 'And wouldn't it be very rude to leave one of your father's guests here alone?' He quirked dark brows.

Harrie gave a dismissive shrug. 'I would say that's my father's problem, not mine,' she bit out sharply. 'I didn't invite you here, Quinn, so don't attempt to monopolise my attention,' she added cuttingly.

He drew in a hissing breath, his expression coldly arrogant now. 'You're excused, Harrie,' he snapped icily.

Her eyes flashed deeply green as she looked across at him. 'Don't start ordering me about, Quinn,' she rasped. 'I'm not one of your minions!'

His mouth quirked in a humourless smile. 'Harrie, I wouldn't employ you if you were the last lawyer left in the world!'

She gasped. 'Why, you—'

'And I have to say, Harrie,' he continued mildly, 'that although there are a lot of things I *do* like about you— your temper isn't one of them! Apart from the fact that it makes you look more beautiful than ever, that lack of control also hints at a recklessness in your nature that would be totally unacceptable in the banking world. You—'

'I think you've already made yourself more than clear,' Harrie burst out angrily, the colour in her cheeks from anger now rather than her embarrassment of earlier.

And this last week she had fought against what she'd believed was her attraction towards this man...! But not any more! He was arrogant, condescending, totally lacking in humour—

She was being unfair now, and she knew that she was. But Quinn seemed to have the power to hurt or annoy her with just a few misplaced words. If they were misplaced...?

'I'm sure we will meet again at dinner, Quinn,' she said stiltedly. 'But other than that I'm sure we can manage to stay out of each other's way for the rest of the weekend!' She turned on her heel and marched briskly out of the room, closing the door firmly behind her.

Only to lean weakly back against it, her vision becoming blurred as the hot tears flooded her eyes.

But what had she expected? That after Monday evening the two of them would fall into each other's arms when they saw each other again? She didn't want that anyway—so why did she feel so hurt and upset that Quinn had shown himself to be so emotionally detached?

Because *she* wasn't, damn it. She only wished that she were!

But somehow—and she had no idea how, when she and Quinn seemed to do nothing but argue every time they met!—Quinn McBride had stepped into her life and refused to leave.

And her heart...?

CHAPTER EIGHT

QUINN watched Harrie with a jaundiced eye as she circulated unhurriedly about the room, stopping to chat to each of the guests gathered in the sitting-room for a pre-dinner drink, her occasional husky laugh grating on his already ragged nerve-endings.

She reminded him of a butterfly, flitting from flower to flower, never stopping for long, but moving steadfastly on before she could be drawn into a lengthy conversation.

She looked like a butterfly too, Quinn thought dourly, a red admiral, her hair looking almost black against the blazing red of the short dress that clung so lovingly to the willowy curves of her body.

And not once, he acknowledged frustratedly, had her gaze so much as rested on him as he'd stood alone near the window, that flitting she was doing from group to group of people never including him.

'Dear, dear, dear, Mr McBride, what have you done to annoy my big sister?' an amused voice drawled mockingly at his side.

Quinn turned sharply to find Danie Summer, the middle daughter, had quietly come to stand beside him, looking the exact opposite of Harrie, her long hair blazing fiery-red down her spine, her short black dress clinging no less lovingly to her own slender curves.

More surprising, she was actually smiling at him! Last weekend she'd been decidedly unfriendly, Quinn remembered with an inward grimace, and in the circumstances—that of being totally ignored by Harrie!—he found the change in Danie more than welcome. Even if her opening remark had been about Harrie!

'Nothing—as far as I'm aware,' he answered dryly.

Danie shook her head mockingly. 'Our daddy told us it was very naughty to tell a lie!' She quirked mocking auburn brows.

Quinn chuckled huskily at this completely unexpected sense of humour from a woman he had hitherto thought bossy to the point of rudeness. 'And your father was quite right to do so,' Quinn happily joined in the slightly flirtatious conversation.

Anything was better than standing here on his own glowering across the room at Harrie! A Harrie who now seemed to have stopped flitting, and was deep in conversation with a tall, rather distinguished-looking, silver-blond-haired man. Damn it, she seemed to be attracted to blond-haired men!

And his inattentiveness was unfair to Danie, who, in truth, didn't have to talk to him at all if she didn't want to. Despite 'her daddy's' efforts to teach his daughters good manners!

'The truth of the matter is, Danie—' he sighed, dragging his attention away from Harrie and the man she was animatedly talking to '—your "big sister" just doesn't like me!' He grimaced.

She took a thoughtful sip of her champagne. 'No?'

Quinn shrugged. 'Afraid not.'

'And, of course—' Danie gave a derisive smile '—you have no idea why that is?'

Oh, he knew exactly why that was; Harrie hadn't liked him before Monday evening, but she had even less reason to do so after that! Not only had his actions shown Harrie what an utter bastard Richard Heaton was, but he had as quickly shown her he was no better by attempting to make love to her himself. Rather a lot for Harrie to forgive him for, he acknowledged heavily. And she obviously hadn't succeeded!

If she had even tried…!

'I could take a pretty accurate guess as to why,' he answered Danie ruefully. 'But I'm not about to bore you with the details,' he added dryly as he saw the speculative glint in her eyes. Eyes, he noticed for the first time, the same colour emerald as her older sister…

Quinn wondered vaguely whether the youngest sister, Andie, would have those same drowning green eyes… He obviously wasn't about to find out tonight; Rome had grimly made his youngest daughter's excuses for dinner when he'd entered the room five minutes ago. But as Rome had very blue eyes, the sisters' emerald green must have come from their mother. If they had also inherited their mother's beauty, as Rome claimed they had, then it was no wonder Rome had been so determined to win her all those years ago!

'But, I can assure you, I wouldn't be bored,' Danie teased.

He gave a humourless smile. 'Nevertheless…'

'I could take a guess myself on it having something to do with the treacherous Richard Heaton,' Danie said disgustedly.

Quinn raised dark brows. 'You know about him?'

Danie smiled, green eyes laughing at his surprise. 'Sisters, especially ones who have been without their mother for ten years—' she sobered slightly '—tend to rely on—confide in—each other more than they would normally. I knew weeks ago that Harrie was seeing Richard Heaton,' she added scathingly. 'Not exactly my type. Too smoothly charming.' She grimaced. 'But he seemed okay.' She shrugged. 'It hurt Harrie pretty badly that he turned out to be such a rat,' she added dismissively.

Quinn wasn't sure he wanted to hear this. In fact, he

knew he didn't. The last thing he needed to know was how much Harrie was still hurting from Richard Heaton's betrayal.

But if the sisters were as close as Danie claimed they were…he couldn't help wondering whether Harrie had also 'confided' anything concerning him to Danie…?

Danie smiled as she astutely read his thoughts. 'As a matter of fact, no,' she murmured slowly, looking at him speculatively over the rim of her glass as she took another sip of her champagne. 'Which, in itself, is very interesting,' she added enigmatically.

'It is?' Quinn attempted to prompt casually—and failed miserably, he knew as he saw Danie's smile widen. The trouble was, there was nothing in the least 'casual' about his feelings towards Harrie.

'Oh, yes,' Danie confirmed lightly. 'I don't— My big sister is about to join us,' she muttered warningly under her breath. 'Why don't you try looking as if you find me wildly interesting—and see what happens?' she suggested wickedly.

Quinn couldn't help laughing at the impishly taunting smile she threw his way before turning to warmly greet her sister. There was obviously much more to Danie Summer than he had first realised!

Although he didn't give that realisation another thought as he also turned to look at Harrie, his own expression defensively wary. Which was probably as well, Harrie returning that gaze with cold disdain!

'Still here, Quinn?' she said sharply.

He drew in a harsh breath at her deliberate rudeness. 'As I'm sure you're well aware, I'm your father's guest, not yours!' he snapped pointedly.

And then wished he had held on to his temper. How could he ever hope to get close to Harrie again if they argued every time they met…?

'I'm sorry,' he bit out abruptly. 'That was uncalled for.'

'I believe that's your cue to apologise for your own rudeness…?' Danie told her sister pointedly.

'Shut up, Danie,' Harrie snapped irritably, looking relieved when Audrey chose that moment to announce it was time for them all to go in to dinner.

'In that case—' Danie linked her arm with Quinn's '—you won't mind if Quinn takes me in to dinner, will you?' She quirked auburn brows at her older sister.

'Why on earth should I mind?' Harrie scorned. 'I've already promised Adam that I shall go in to dinner with him,' she announced with satisfaction, leaving them, to bestow a glowing smile on the distinguished-looking man she'd been talking to a few minutes ago.

Quinn scowled as, having returned to the other man's side, Harrie linked her arm as intimately with his as Danie was now doing with his own.

'Careful, Quinn,' Danie drawled softly at his side, 'your jealousy is starting to show!'

'Jealousy!' he snapped angrily. 'I would like to tan her backside!'

Danie laughed softly as the two of them strolled through to the dining-room. 'I wouldn't give her being with Adam another thought; we've all known him for years,' she added dismissively.

Quinn still thought Harrie could have stood a little further away from the other man, and she certainly didn't have to pull her chair that intimately close to his as the two of them sat across and slightly down the table from Danie and himself in the dining-room!

Damn it, his jealousy wasn't just showing; it was eating him alive!

'You've probably heard of him,' Danie continued conversationally as she saw he was still distracted by the other couple. 'Adam Munroe,' she supplied at Quinn's frowning look.

Adam Munroe! The Adam Munroe?

'The film producer?' he prompted as lightly as he felt able—which came out more as a grating of teeth!

'The one and only,' Danie confirmed brightly.

Quinn looked across at the other man with new eyes. There was no doubting that the other man would be attractive to women, with that blond hair shot through with silver, an aristocratically handsome face, and possessed of an air of cynicism that probably owed nothing to his late thirties in age but more to the world of film-making where he had made his fortune.

A film producer or a banker! Could the two men really be further apart, in career as well as in looks?

And there was no doubting which of the two Harrie found the more exciting as her husky laugh rang out once again!

Quinn sighed. 'I suppose it's too much to hope that he's already married?'

'A bachelor through and through.' Danie laughed at Quinn's expense. 'He's a friend of Daddy's, Quinn,' she added in a bored voice, obviously not impressed herself, either by the other man's looks or profession. 'Oh, for goodness' sake, Quinn, Adam has known us all since we had pigtails and braces on our teeth!' she assured him impatiently.

Quinn looked at her with raised brows as her smile showed him a row of even white teeth. 'I commend your orthodontist,' he murmured dryly, having a problem associating either Harrie or Danie with pigtails let alone braces on their teeth; they were both such beautiful women, in a totally individual way, it was difficult to imagine either of them any other way!

'Forget the orthodontist,' Danie snapped with some of

her old sharpness. 'The point I'm trying to make, Quinn, is that Adam no more has a romantic interest in Harrie than she does in him. The two of them are just playing the socially polite game of flirtation!' she added exasperatedly as he continued to look less than convinced.

Quinn understood her exasperation with him, wished he could believe what she was saying. But as dinner progressed, and he watched the couple on the other side of the table seeming completely engrossed in each other, he found it very hard to accept.

Not that Danie wasn't an entertaining dining companion herself, telling him several funny anecdotes, edged, of course, with that sarcastic asperity that seemed such a part of her nature. She even made him laugh a couple of times—which was a feat in itself when he felt so little like laughing.

But all the time he listened or spoke to Danie he was aware of Harrie sitting further down the table. And, from her complete preoccupation with Adam Munroe, she was no longer even aware of Quinn's presence in the room!

Quinn and Danie, Harrie silently accused inside—even as she appeared to listen attentively to what Adam was saying.

She wouldn't have believed it if she hadn't witnessed it with her own eyes. Oh, not that she thought Danie was serious in the flirtation; she knew her sister's views on meaningless relationships too well to believe that. But the same couldn't be said for Quinn; Harrie had no doubts that he had meaningless relationships off to a fine art!

What was he trying to do? she fumed inwardly. Work his way through the Summer sisters, until one of them actually fell into his arms? Well, as far as she was concerned he was going to have a long wait, and Andie was in no fit state to be charmed by anyone. Which brought her back to Danie…

But her younger sister certainly seemed to be enjoying herself, Harrie noticed with a frown…

'Your father was telling me earlier that Andie isn't well again?'

It took tremendous effort on Harrie's part to drag her attention back to what Adam had just said, her head full of visions of one day having to welcome Quinn into the family—as her brother-in-law!

'Harrie…?' Adam prompted gently.

Pull yourself together, Harrie, she instructed herself firmly. Quinn and Danie were only talking together—not making wedding plans!

'She has the flu,' she answered Adam distractedly.

He made a face. 'I thought Rome said that was what was wrong with her last weekend, which was the reason she was unable to be at the Summer Fête…?'

The Summer Fête… The scene of her first meeting with Quinn McBride. Was that really only a week ago…?

'It was,' Harrie confirmed inattentively, having noticed now that Danie and Quinn had both refused coffee, excusing themselves from the table to stroll out of the dining-room together.

To go where? she frowned.

Despite the fact that Quinn was—as he'd reminded her all too forcefully earlier!—her father's guest, Harrie had secretly believed—hoped?—Quinn had really come here to see her again.

Idiot! she chided herself disgustedly. So Quinn had kissed her on Monday. Maybe more than kissed her, she allowed grudgingly. That didn't mean it had meant anything to him.

As it had to her…?

She shied away from such a thought. Just because Quinn

had now turned his attention to Danie was no reason for her to feel—to feel what? Hurt? Betrayed? *Jealous?*

'Actually, Harrie, you don't look too well yourself,' Adam said concernedly as he looked at her closely.

'Really, Adam,' she replied teasingly. 'That is hardly gallant! But as it happens—' she sobered, taking pity on him as he looked a little sheepish at the rebuke '—I'm still recovering from a throat infection.'

And a bruised heart?

But who'd done the bruising?

There was no doubting the fact that she had felt a fool over her mistake concerning Richard, but she'd reasoned that out over this last week, and had realised, from the hurtful things Richard had said to her on Monday evening, that he'd just been using her, that as Rome Summer's daughter she had opened doors for him that might otherwise have been closed. Harrie had also realised that the man she'd thought herself in love with simply didn't exist.

But there was still an unexplainable ache in her heart—which had nothing whatsoever to do with Richard.

And everything to do with Quinn McBride…?

A lot of good that was going to do her, when he now seemed to have transferred his interest to Danie!

What was *wrong* with her? She couldn't be in love with Quinn—could she…?

Of course not, she told herself firmly. Love happened slowly, between two people who liked each other, who enjoyed each other's company—it didn't come bursting into your life riding roughshod over everything, and everyone, else in your life. Certainly not in the guise of Quinn McBride!

That decided, she turned attentively to Adam. 'Would you like to take a stroll outside in the garden?'

He raised blond brows. 'This is all very sudden, Miss Summer.' He pretended to be shocked by her invitation.

Harrie gave him a playful punch on the shoulder. 'Don't be ridiculous, Adam,' she dismissed easily. 'I'm not one of your impressionable actresses; my invitation for a walk in the garden meant exactly that!'

'I know.' Adam sighed his disappointment, standing up to pull back her chair for her, and the two of them strolled over to make their excuses to Harrie's father. 'If I'm ever in need of having my feet planted firmly back on the ground, I just pay the Summer sisters a visit; you never hesitate to let me know just how unimpressed you all are!'

Harrie laughed huskily. 'I'm glad we're useful for something!' Having reached her father, she bent down to kiss him lightly on the cheek. 'Adam is taking me outside for a romantic stroll in the garden,' she excused with a teasing grin in Adam's direction.

Her father looked slightly perplexed. 'I've given up even trying to keep up with you girls.' He shook his head. 'Just make sure you tell me when any of you decide to get married—and to whom!' he added disgustedly.

Adam kept a light hold on her elbow as they walked outside. 'What was all that about?' he prompted, frowning.

Harrie gave a dismissive shrug, having no intention of explaining any of the circumstances of this last week to this friend of the family. Although she was in no doubt herself as to what her father was alluding to: Danie, and not herself, was the daughter who'd left the room with Quinn, and now Harrie was going outside with Adam. No wonder Rome was confused!

But it was not conducive, to a stroll or anything else, when the two of them walked out onto the patio to find Danie and Quinn sitting there together in the semi-darkness!

Harrie stiffened at the sight of her sister sitting so close beside Quinn on one of the wicker sofas. But at least they vere only sitting together, she reasoned a few seconds ater; it could have been much worse!

Quinn stood up abruptly at their approach, his eyes glittering brightly in the semi-darkness of the summer evening, although he made no effort to speak.

Harrie didn't know what to say, either. Which was odd n itself; she usually had plenty to say to Quinn!

'You're looking particularly handsome this evening, Adam,' Danie drawled as she stood up beside Quinn to kiss the other man lightly on the cheek.

Harrie frowned; was that a mocking glance Danie also shot in Quinn's direction? And if it were, for what reason?

'Let's take it as said that we all look wonderful this evening,' Adam derided dismissively, looking curiously at Quinn.

Of course, the two men probably hadn't been introduced, Harrie realised belatedly. Well, that was easily rectified.

'Adam Munroe. Quinn McBride.' Her voice hardened slightly over the second name, giving a slight shiver as Quinn turned to look at her with arctic-blue eyes.

What was wrong with him? She was the one who'd made a fool of herself earlier in the week, not him, so why should he be looking at her so accusingly? Besides, it hadn't taken him long to find someone else to flirt with!

'Cold, love?' Adam noticed her shiver concernedly, putting an altogether wrong interpretation on it. 'Here, take my jacket—'

'No!' Harrie protested as he began to shrug out of the pristine black evening jacket. 'I'm not cold. Really,' she assured him hastily as she could see he wasn't convinced. There was a dangerous glitter in Quinn's gaze as he watched the exchange—a gaze she was unable to meet!

'Perhaps we should go back inside, anyway.' Adam still

frowned. 'There's a slight chill in the air, and we don't want your throat infection to flare up again.'

Her five-day course of antibiotics had already taken care of that. But the suggestion they go back inside, in view of the fact that Danie and Quinn were out here too, sounded like a good one to Harrie...

'No, we certainly wouldn't want that, would we?' Quinn rasped harshly before she could answer Adam.

Harrie gave him a sharp look. Why on earth was he so angry? Okay, so she hadn't exactly been polite to him earlier, but they weren't exactly polite to each other most of the time, were they?

'It is getting a little chilly; why don't we all go back inside to the library and have a nightcap together?' Danie put in lightly.

Harrie shot her sister an accusing look. What was Danie playing at? Her sister knew exactly what had happened between Richard and herself earlier this week, and the part Quinn had played in it—which meant Danie also had to know that a cosy nightcap with Quinn, a witness to her humiliation, was the last thing she wanted!

'An excellent idea.' Adam instantly accepted the suggestion. 'The beauties of nature have never been high on my list of "have-to-sees"!' he explained dryly.

Adam had never made any secret of the fact that he found the removal of his friend Rome, along with his wife and three daughters, to this country estate bizarre in the extreme. He was a townie to his fingertips, and the last twenty years of visiting them at Summer Manor hadn't changed Adam's opinion of the countryside one iota!

Danie laughed at his obvious aversion, moving to link her arm with his. 'Come along, my poor pet,' she drawled tauntingly, 'I'll take you back inside, away from the horrible moths and flies!'

Harrie watched disbelievingly as her sister strolled back

into the house with Adam—leaving her alone outside with Quinn!

She looked up at him beneath lowered lashes, stiffening resentfully as she saw he was looking at her warily. What did he think she was going to do now that the two of them were alone in the moonlight: pounce on him?

'Come along, Quinn,' she snapped, turning away. 'It seems we're about to have a nightcap together!' But before she'd managed to walk two steps she found her arm grasped as she was turned roughly back to face him.

'You certainly haven't wasted any time, have you?' Quinn grated scornfully. 'You've given "off with the old, on with the new" a completely new meaning as far as I'm concerned!'

'What on earth—?' she gasped as Quinn's fingers dug painfully into her arms that were still covered in the bruises inflicted by Richard.

'Munroe!' Quinn bit out with distaste.

Her eyes widened at the unmistakable accusation. 'Are you saying—? Implying—?'

'Both of those things,' he confirmed disgustedly. 'And I've been feeling like a heel this last week because I kissed you on Monday evening!' He shook his head. 'I should have pressed home my advantage when I had the chance!'

Harrie could feel herself pale, staring up at him with dark green eyes. 'You're fooling yourself if you believe you ever *had* the advantage, Quinn,' she told him dully.

'Am I?' he scorned, his aqua-blue eyes glittering down at her with dislike. 'Maybe. But maybe not. As the experience will never be repeated, we'll never know the answer to that, will we?' He thrust her away from him. 'I'll wish you a pleasant night, Harrie,' he added. 'Make my excuses to your sister concerning the nightcap, will you? If I have to be with you a minute longer I think it would choke me!'

He turned sharply on his heel and strode forcefully back into the house.

Harrie dropped down weakly into one of the wicker patio chairs, her face buried in her hands.

Quinn despised her. It had been there in his expression, in his eyes, in his words and the tone of his voice.

Quinn despised her—and she—she *loved* him!

She'd been wrong, so very wrong. Liking didn't always come first. Love didn't always grow between two people who were already friends.

Because she loved Quinn, ached with loving him. And he'd just made it quite clear that he despised her...!

CHAPTER NINE

HE HAD slept badly, Quinn acknowledged with a groan as he opened one eye to look at the bedside clock, and saw it was only seven-thirty. The time he usually woke up at home to go to work!

Except he wasn't at home, was still at the Summer estate. Although he wished himself a hundred miles away from here...!

It had been barely ten o'clock when he'd retired to his room the evening before, and, after pacing those confines for well over an hour, he'd finally given up, making his way quietly down the wide staircase, in the hope of being unobserved by any of the guests who'd still been downstairs, before leaving the house completely to go for a walk in the chilly evening air.

It had done little to improve his chances of sleeping, his mind consumed with thoughts of Harrie. As she had last looked.

As if he had just hit her...!

And in a way, he had, he'd realised as he'd walked away from the house. His last words to her had been chosen deliberately to hurt.

As he'd been hurting all evening as he'd watched her with Adam Munroe...?

Damn it, yes!

He couldn't bear the thought of any other man being near her, talking to her, let alone hearing her laughing with them. Because—as he'd acknowledged somewhere around one o'clock this morning, as he'd walked back through the neighbouring wood trying to find his way back to the

145

house—he wanted all of that for himself. He wanted *Harrie* for himself!

He sat up in the bed with a groan, swinging his legs to the floor, his expression despondent. What was he going to do about these feelings he had for Harrie? What could he do? Because there was no doubting that, after last night, he had totally alienated her. He would be lucky if she ever spoke to him again, let alone anything else!

Even one of her insults would be welcome at the moment, Quinn decided ruefully.

He stood up abruptly as he heard the sound of voices down on the driveway outside through his partly open window, arriving at that window just in time to see Danie standing on the gravel below, watching Harrie as she rode away on the back of a huge black horse.

Quinn watched Harrie too, admiring the way she sat on the huge animal as if she were a part of it, bent low over the horse's neck, her long dark hair streaming out behind her.

He hadn't realised she could ride. But, then, there were still a lot of things he didn't know about Harrie! Or was ever likely to find out now...?

'Why don't you come down and join me for coffee?'

Quinn turned sharply from where he'd just watched Harrie, sitting confidently astride the horse, as she disappeared amongst the trees he'd been temporarily lost in last night. Obviously she wasn't going to have the same problem...

Danie grinned up at him as he looked down at her, her hand over her eyes to shield them from the dazzling bright sunshine. 'Come down and have some coffee with me,' she invited again lightly. 'But put some clothes on first, hmm?' she added derisively.

Quinn became instantly aware of the fact that he was standing at the window, in full view of anyone who cared to look up, wearing only a pair of black underpants! And that Danie, with a display of her usual wicked sense of humour, was now laughing at his obvious discomfort at that fact!

He held up an acknowledging hand. 'I'll be down in a few minutes,' he agreed dryly.

Danie nodded. 'I'll keep the coffee warm!'

One thing he was quickly learning to do, when around the acerbic Danie Summer, was to laugh at himself, Quinn acknowledged as he went through to the adjoining bathroom to take a shower. If he didn't, she would do it for him!

'I would offer you more than coffee—' Danie shrugged when Quinn joined her in the otherwise deserted breakfast-room fifteen minutes later '—but it's Sunday, and we all have to wait until everyone else is up, and the other guests arrive, before we can have brunch.' Her grimace of disgust showed exactly what she thought of that arrangement.

'Coffee will be fine,' Quinn accepted as he sat down opposite her; after his lack of sleep last night he couldn't even bear the thought of food at the moment!

'In case you were worried earlier,' Danie drawled, holding out a steaming cup of coffee to him, 'Harrie has been riding almost since she could walk.'

Quinn kept his expression deliberately bland; this young lady was far too astute to allow his barriers to slip! 'I wasn't worried,' he told Danie truthfully; it was obvious, even to a novice like himself, that Harrie was a first-class horsewoman.

Danie arched auburn brows. 'No?'

'No,' Quinn informed dryly. 'Danie, exactly why do you think that I would be in the least worried about Harrie riding that huge black monster?' he derided.

'His name is Ebony,' Danie corrected firmly. 'And the

reason I thought you might be worried about Harrie is because you're in love with her.'

Quinn almost choked over the sip of hot coffee he had been in the process of taking. He swallowed it down as he stared disbelievingly at Danie, stunned by the boldness of the statement she had just made.

In love with Harrie!

He was?

'Correct me if I'm wrong,' Danie commenced slowly, 'but—'

'You're wrong!' Quinn cut in firmly before she could say anything else to shake him. Although that last remark must rate a ten on the Richter scale!

Because there was no doubting Danie had shaken him with that casually made statement. Because he'd never been in love with any woman. And he certainly wasn't in love with the prickly Harrie Summer now!

He wanted her. Desired her. To the point where he didn't want any other man near her, he admitted... But that didn't mean he was *in love with her*, damn it!

'What conclusions did you just come to?' Danie asked him interestedly, obviously having watched him as he'd digested the possibility of being in love with Harrie—and as quickly dismissed it as being ridiculous! 'It doesn't matter.' She sighed dismissively. 'I thought I was stubborn.' Danie shook her head disgustedly. 'But you two are much worse.'

'Two?' Quinn prompted as lightly as he was able.

'Two,' Danie confirmed scathingly. 'Harrie won't admit—to me, at any rate!—that she's in love with you, either!'

Quinn swallowed hard, carefully putting his cup back down on its saucer before answering. 'Maybe that's because she isn't.' He shrugged.

'Rubbish,' Danie scorned.

Quinn couldn't help grinning at her disgusted expression. 'I wouldn't change your profession and take up matchmaking, if I were you,' he teased. 'You would make a complete hash of it!'

'Very funny!' Danie wrinkled her nose at him. 'You—'

'This looks very cosy,' rasped a harsh voice. 'Would it be too much of an interruption if I joined you for a cup of coffee?'

Quinn had looked up sharply at the sound of Harrie's voice, a shutter coming down over his inner thoughts as he took in how beautiful she looked after her early morning ride. Her hair was loose and tangled down her back, her eyes sparkled, and there was a healthy glow in her cheeks. A little like how she would look when making love, he thought achingly.

'Of course you can join us,' Danie assured her sister warmly. 'I don't think anyone else is awake yet,' she dismissed, pouring out the third cup of coffee and pushing it across the table to the place next to where Quinn sat.

He looked with narrowed eyes at the mischief-making redhead, knowing she had deliberately put the coffee there so that Harrie had to sit next to him. But he should have realised, as should Danie—with Harrie there was no 'had to' about anything!

'Thanks.' Harrie leant forward and moved the coffee-cup to the end of the table—as far away from Quinn as it was possible for her to sit! 'I'm a bit hot and sticky after my morning ride,' she gruffly excused the reason for her distance, before burying her face in the coffee-cup.

Danie grinned across at Quinn knowingly. 'Of course you are,' she acknowledged dryly before standing up. 'I hope you'll both excuse me; I have a few things to do for Rome before brunch.'

Quinn watched frustratedly as Danie turned and left the room. Damn it, she had done it again: manoeuvred him into a situation—as she had outside in the garden last night—and then just walked off and left him alone with Harrie. A Harrie, he was sure, who certainly didn't want to be alone with him!

Harrie lowered her coffee-cup slowly, her expression wary as she looked across at him with apprehensive green eyes.

An apprehension he had put there last night, Quinn realised, when he'd been so insulting to her. Damn it, Harrie was the last person he wanted to hurt—and the one person that he constantly seemed to be doing so!

Neither of them spoke after Danie's departure, the seconds slowly slipping past, the silence stretching awkwardly between them, the atmosphere becoming more and more tense.

This was ridiculous, Quinn finally decided. But the reason for the tension was mainly his own doing, he also acknowledged...

He gave a deep sigh. 'I believe I owe you yet another apology,' he bit out tautly.

Harrie raised dark brows uninterestedly. 'You do?' She frowned.

'Yes,' he rasped. 'I said some pretty—damning things, to you last night. And—'

'Actually, I would say they were more insulting than damning,' Harrie interrupted softly, slowly putting down her coffee-cup. 'But there was probably a lot of truth in what you said, too,' she added dryly.

Quinn frowned. 'You mean you are involved with Munroe?' Surely Danie hadn't been wrong about that situation, after all...? His chest tightened, and his hands clenched under the table just at the thought of it!

Harrie gave a softly humourless laugh. 'No, I don't mean that at all,' she dismissed. 'I'm no more Adam's type than he is mine. Adam likes his women small, fluffy, and dependent. I think you would agree, Quinn—' she quirked dark brows at him mockingly '—that I'm out on all three counts!'

As she was five feet eight inches tall in her bare feet, with a very determined nature, and an independence that bordered on arrogance, Quinn would have to say he did agree! But, then, up until a week ago, Harrie wouldn't have been his type, either! Things, and people, changed...

Because Harrie was certainly 'his type' now—in fact, she made every other woman seem insipid and uninteresting in comparison!

'What I meant, Quinn,' Harrie continued heavily at his silence, 'was that, in retrospect, it must have looked as if I were flirting with Adam yesterday evening.' She grimaced. 'The truth of the matter is I've been feeling a little...raw, since—well, since Richard, and maybe I did overreact with Adam last night.' She avoided his gaze. 'To put it in Danie's words, I was "all over the man"!'

Danie again. He'd actually come to like the other woman over the last twelve hours or so—but that didn't alter the fact that she had a way of saying things that would be better left unsaid!

And if Harrie had needed to 'overreact' with some man, why couldn't it have been him?

He shook his head, smiling ruefully. 'I shouldn't take too much notice of what Danie says, if I were you,' he drawled. 'She's great fun to be with, but her powers of observation aren't very accurate!' On two counts that he knew of: he wasn't in love with Harrie—and she most definitely wasn't in love with him! '"All over the man" sounds like an exaggeration to me,' he added dismissively.

Over-friendly more adequately described it, he decided. Although last night, before he'd had time to calm down, he would probably have agreed with Danie's summing up of the situation...! In fact, he had!

'It does?' Harrie said hopefully.

'Yes.' Quinn smiled reassuringly.

'Thank heavens for that!' Harrie gave a relieved sigh.
'After what Danie said earlier, I was beginning to wonder
how I would ever be able to face Adam again,' she added
ruefully.

Face *Adam*...! What about him? Obviously he didn't
even come into the equation, Quinn realised angrily.

'Thanks for the coffee and conversation,' Harrie said
lightly, standing up. 'I had better go up to my room now,
I need to shower and change before the others start to come
down.'

Before Adam came down, Quinn muttered to himself
once Harrie had left the breakfast-room!

Damn it, on top of everything else, he was talking to
himself now!

Since meeting Harrie Summer he'd found himself doing
lots of things he'd never done before, such as insulting a
woman, kissing her against her will, and, worst of all—
chasing after her!

And Harrie Summer was that woman!

As quickly as it had risen, his anger abated. There had
to be a reason he was acting so out of character. But the
only reason he could come up with was so unbelievable
that it left him paralysed with shock.

Could Danie be right...? Could he be in love with
Harrie...?

Harrie breathed a sigh of relief once she was outside in
the hallway. But she didn't linger there, hurrying up to the
privacy of her bedroom, closing the door thankfully behind
her.

Her first instinct, on arriving back in the house after her
ride and hearing the sound of Danie and Quinn's voices

coming from the breakfast-room, had been to go quietly up to her bedroom before they realised she was there.

Her second instinct had told her not to be such a coward, that she would have to face Quinn again some time today, and maybe it would be better if it were done now, with only Danie as a witness.

She'd received a jolt to her confidence when she'd seen how relaxed Danie and Quinn looked in each other's company, the two of them laughing together over something as she'd entered the breakfast-room. And why shouldn't they enjoy each other's company? Before leaving for her ride, Harrie had very firmly told Danie that she had absolutely no romantic interest in Quinn.

Leaving the way clear for Danie with Quinn if that was what her sister decided she wanted...?

And hadn't Quinn just told her that he found Danie 'fun to be with'...?

Something Harrie was sure he didn't find her. But, then, there hadn't been that much for her to laugh about since she'd first met Quinn! Not that that was Quinn's fault; he wasn't responsible for the fact that Richard had turned out to be such a swine. It just meant that she and Quinn had started off badly—and it had deteriorated from there, she acknowledged with a groan.

Quinn found Danie 'fun to be with'...

Those words kept going round and round in her head until she could have screamed. Danie was fun, the two of them the best of friends as well as sisters—but that didn't mean Harrie could ever sit back and watch Danie and Quinn together.

But what choice would she have if that was the way things turned out?

None, she realised achingly.

Her tears mingled with the shower water as she stood under the punishing spray. She couldn't—wouldn't—compete with her own sister for the man she loved. Besides, Quinn himself had shown a decided preference for her beautiful and witty sister.

She would have to get through today as best she could, Harrie finally decided. The future—especially one that might include Danie and Quinn being together!—would have to wait.

But it didn't help in that decision that the first people she saw, when she came outside onto the sun-warm patio to greet their guests before brunch, were David Hampton and Corinne Westley—Quinn's sister!

Rome hadn't mentioned that he'd invited the other couple here today—but, then, he hadn't told her he had invited Quinn for the weekend, either!

'Harrie!' Corinne greeted her warmly, obviously relaxed and happy now the tension of the last few weeks was at last over, looking glowingly beautiful in a sun-dress the exact colour of her aqua-blue eyes.

Quinn's eyes...

Harrie mentally shook herself, returning the other woman's smile as she tried to push thoughts of Quinn from her mind. Which wasn't very easy when confronted with his sister!

'It's lovely to see you both again,' she murmured politely as David bent to kiss her lightly on the cheek.

'And under such different circumstances.' Corinne squeezed her hands warmly in recognition of the part she believed Harrie had played in that change of circumstances.

'Quinn is around somewhere,' Harrie told the other woman noncommittally, feeling rather guilty at the other woman's obvious gratitude. Corinne still had no idea that until five days ago Richard Heaton had been a friend of hers—and Harrie would rather it remained that way!

The fewer people that knew of that particular stupidity on her part, the better!

There were already a dozen or so guests sitting down in the wicker chairs, or standing around on the patio, chatting easily together. But a quick look round showed Harrie that neither Danie or Quinn were here yet. Because they were somewhere together...?

'Have you said hello to Rome yet?' she prompted forcefully, having spotted her father a short distance away as he chatted easily with Adam.

'When we arrived,' David confirmed easily.

Now what did she do with them? Harrie frowned. Not that she didn't think the smoothly confident politician and the beautiful Corinne couldn't very well take care of themselves in any social situation; it was just that as their host's daughter she felt an obligation not to just walk away and leave them to it! But, in actual fact, Quinn's sister was the last person she wanted to talk to.

'Come and meet Adam Munroe,' she suggested lightly, not feeling she was being too unfair to Adam; he always liked to be introduced to a beautiful woman, and Corinne was certainly that!

The five of them were chatting comfortably together when Harrie saw Quinn's arrival onto the patio. Actually, she had felt him there before she saw him, experiencing a tingling sensation down the length of her spine that made her turn and look in Quinn's direction.

Just Quinn. There was no Danie at his side.

She smiled her relief, turning back to make her excuses to the others before strolling over to greet Quinn. 'Corinne and David have arrived,' she told him unnecessarily, sure he must have seen his sister and her fiancé standing beside her father and Adam when he'd glanced across at their group a few seconds ago.

But she had to find something to say to him; she was

determined he should never guess at this second—even
more devastating!—folly of hers. And loving a man a
detached as she knew Quinn McBride to be had to be he
biggest folly of all!

'Really?' He scowled, looking around irritatedly until
he saw Corinne and David talking to Rome. 'I had no idea
they were going to be here,' he muttered grimly.

And that he wasn't pleased by the fact was obvious. But
why wasn't he? Harrie wondered. Her father was exactly
the sort of wealthy and influential man David Hampton
should cultivate if he were intent on getting to the top in
politics. Besides, after the way her father had helped
Corinne last weekend, it was only natural that the three of
them should meet up at some time...

She turned to look at Quinn searchingly. Only to find
him looking down at her as intently, those aqua-blue eyes
narrowed, and as unfathomable as the sea they resembled

'Quinn, what is it?' she burst out when she could stand
the rapidly building tension between them no longer.

A nerve pulsed in his rigidly clenched jaw. 'I need to
talk to you,' he finally rasped.

Her frown deepened as she searched the hard planes of
his face for some sign of what he needed to talk to her
about. But she was wasting her time; his eyes were icy as
an arctic sky, and his expression was as coldly unreadable

'What about?' she prompted agitatedly.

He looked about them restlessly at the socially relaxed
people milling about the patio. 'Not here,' he finally
ground out. 'Could we go somewhere else? Somewhere
where we won't be disturbed?' he added harshly.

'What is it?' Her agitation increased, her hand moving
to the hardness of his arm.

It couldn't be anything to do with her father; he was
obviously his normal charming self as he talked with
Corinne and David. And it couldn't be Andie, because she

vas still in bed suffering from the after-effects of her illness. Which only left Danie...

Or Richard...?

'What's he done now?' she gasped, feeling her face pale.

'Who?' Quinn frowned his irritation. 'What are you talking about, Harrie? I said I wanted to talk to you; it doesn't involve anyone else.'

Danie, then, she accepted heavily.

Did the fact that he'd kissed her a couple of times give Quinn the impression he owed her some sort of explanation now that his interest had transferred to her sister? Because there was no way she was going 'somewhere where they wouldn't be disturbed' just so that she could listen to Quinn telling her how he now felt about Danie!

'Do stop looking so grim, Quinn.' She made her tone deliberately taunting. 'I hope you don't think that I imagine what happened between the two of us—if anything *did* happen,' she added with a dismissive laugh, 'meant anything?' She arched mocking brows.

His arm tensed beneath her touch. 'It didn't?'

'Of course not,' she assured him scornfully, her lips feeling frozen into position as she continued to smile up at him. 'We're both grown-up people, Quinn. And one day, I'm sure, we'll both look back on this little episode and remember it with affection,' she assured him lightly.

He continued to frown down at her, and it took every ounce of self-determination Harrie possessed to continue to meet that piercing gaze. But she would not let Quinn see how this was hurting her. She couldn't. She wasn't going to be left with a lot once he had gone, but the self-respect that had only recently returned to her, was something she was determined to hang on to. It was all she had!

Although she wished Quinn would just finish this conversation and let her quietly slip away—because she

wasn't sure just how much longer she could keep up thi
act!

'I'm glad you feel that way,' Quinn finally rasped. 'Al
though, the same can't be said for—' He broke off, hi
gaze suddenly fixed on something over Harrie's shoulder

Harrie turned sharply to look at the reason for his sud
den distraction. Danie stood in the doorway, silently beck
oning Quinn over to her, her expression anxious.

'Excuse me, won't you?' Quinn murmured vaguely to
Harrie even as he moved towards Danie.

Leaving Harrie with the knowledge that she was neve
going to learn who or what 'the same couldn't be said for'

She stood transfixed as Quinn and Danie talked softly
together in the doorway for a few seconds. Then Quinn
turned abruptly on his heel to stride back into the house
And, after one last anxious glance in Harrie's direction
Danie quickly followed him.

Let them go, Harrie told herself. Obviously Quinn had
made his choice. She would only make matters worse i.
she were to follow them.

And yet...

Something hadn't been quite right about that last lin
gering glance Danie had given her. Her sister hadn't jus
looked anguished, she had seemed angry too.

What was going on...?

She found the answer to that almost as soon as she re-
entered the house, as she followed the sound of raised
voices coming from the sitting-room. Voices she recognised.

Quinn's.

And Richard's...!

CHAPTER TEN

QUINN looked at the younger man with unmistakable dislike. That Heaton had the gall to just turn up here—!

Quinn hadn't been able to believe it when Danie had told him a few minutes ago that Richard Heaton was here, and had marched angrily back inside the house to see for himself.

The younger man looked as confident as ever as he stood at the side of a woman Quinn realised he also recognised.

'I don't need to ask how you wormed your way in here,' Quinn scorned at the other man, his gaze sweeping pointedly over the woman at Heaton's side.

'Mr McBride...?' The woman looked at him dazedly. 'I don't understand what the problem is.' She shook her head. 'Mr Summer invited me down here for Sunday brunch. And, of course, I was thrilled to come.' She shook her head. 'But this young lady seems to feel there's some problem—'

'This "young lady" is Danie Summer,' Danie informed the other woman tautly. 'Rome's daughter.'

'One of them,' Richard Heaton interjected.

'And you aren't the problem—*he* is!' Danie looked vehemently at Richard Heaton.

'Richard is...?' Jane Freeman frowned in confusion. 'But Mr Summer assured me it would be perfectly all right with him if I brought a friend with me. I simply don't understand,' she repeated dazedly as Danie continued to glare at Richard, and Quinn looked ready to hit him!

In fact, Quinn felt quite sorry for the female reporter.

The two of them had first met last Sunday when Jane had come to interview his sister, and Quinn had found her intelligent as well as empathetic. Unfortunately, Jane had had no idea of the real reason she was being asked to write the article on Corinne. Which meant she also had no idea of Richard Heaton's part in any of that, either!

But Richard Heaton knew! As he also knew the havoc he would wreak by his coming here today!

Quinn turned his attention back to the other man, angered anew by the look of challenging insolence on the younger man's face. 'I thought I warned you about making an enemy of Rome Summer...?' he murmured softly.

Richard Heaton shrugged unconcernedly. 'I'm here as Jane's partner for brunch—'

'You're here to make trouble!' Quinn cut in forcefully. 'We both know that. So why don't you—?' He broke off, having become aware of someone else having come to stand in the doorway behind him, turning slowly, dismayed to see Harrie standing there.

She looked as if someone had just slapped her in the face!

Her face was very pale as she stared across the room at Richard Heaton, her eyes looking huge and dark as emeralds in stark contrast.

Damn Heaton, Quinn thought, and far from the first time. Damn the other man to hell!

'Harrie—'

She pushed Quinn's hand away as he would have reached out to her, walking past him, going to stand directly in front of Richard Heaton. 'Get out,' she told him coldly.

If anything the other man's expression became even more insolent. 'I was invited,' he drawled. 'Or, at least, Jane was.' He reached out and slid a possessive arm about the female reporter's shoulders. 'I'm sure I've mentioned

Jane Freeman to you before, Harrie,' he drawled mockingly. 'And Quinn already knows her very well, don't you?' He looked across at Quinn tauntingly.

'Jane Freeman...' Harrie repeated softly, anger flashing in her eyes as she obviously remembered where she had heard that name before. 'You are so low, Richard,' she told him with contempt, shaking her head. 'I can't believe I was ever taken in by you!'

'Richard, you're here as a colleague, nothing else.' Jane Freeman impatiently shook off the heavy weight of his arm about her shoulders. 'Although it seems I've missed something here...' she added.

Richard Heaton raised blond brows. 'Shall I tell her— or would one of you like to?' he taunted.

Quinn felt his hands tighten into fists at his sides. He knew this was Rome's home, that there were a couple of dozen guests not twenty yards away, too—but if this meeting didn't soon come to an end he knew he was going to be unable to stop himself from administering the punch he had wanted to give Richard Heaton for so long. And Quinn knew it was no longer just for what he had done to his sister...

'I don't think any of us need to tell Jane anything.' Surprisingly it was Harrie who answered the other man. 'You've had your fun, Richard,' she continued firmly, 'now I think it's time you just left. Quietly. Don't you...?' she challenged softly.

Quinn had to admire her in that moment. Not only did she sound completely in control of the situation, but she looked magnificent too!

Richard Heaton looked momentarily shaken by her confident calmness too. 'Now, why should I want to do that...?' he murmured slowly, frowning in puzzlement.

Harrie shrugged. 'Because of a contract you've agreed to sign with Leeward Publications on Monday...?' she returned coolly, glancing calmly down at her wrist-watch. 'Tomorrow, in fact.'

Quinn watched as the other man paled. And with good reason. There had been a definite threat behind Harrie's words.

Richard Heaton moistened his lips. 'How do you know about that?' he asked suspiciously.

Harrie raised mocking brows. 'Because I drew up the contract,' she informed him coldly.

Now the younger man looked more than shaken. As well he might, Quinn acknowledged ruefully. He'd just been informed that he had been manoeuvred into a corner—by the very people he had believed he was besting by coming here today!

Quinn looked at Harrie with admiration. He should have known, should have guessed, from the little Rome had been willing to tell him yesterday, that Harrie would also be in on his legal dealings with Richard Heaton. After all, she was Rome's lawyer...

And for Harrie, it would have meant so much more than carrying out her legal duties; Heaton had used her, made a fool of her. God, she was magnificent, Quinn decided.

He only hoped she hadn't overplayed her hand by telling Heaton as much as she had...?

'The contract isn't signed yet,' Richard Heaton reminded with harsh defiance, his top lip turned back in scorn.

'True,' Harrie accepted mildly. 'But I think we both know you will be a fool if you don't sign—don't we?' She quirked mocking brows at him.

Quinn had never admired—loved?—Harrie as much as he did in that moment. She was amazing, unlike any other woman he had ever known. An undoubtedly loving sister and daughter—but a most formidable enemy. And he wanted her for his own!

Richard Heaton's breath left him in a vehement hiss. 'I could still break the real story about the snow-white Corinne,' he sneered.

Quinn tensed, taking a step forward, only to be held in check by Harrie as she turned to give him a briefly reassuring smile.

She turned back to Richard Heaton, giving a humourless laugh. 'Following Jane's article on Monday, you would only make a complete idiot of yourself. You'd come over as a vindictive man harassing a vulnerable woman. Why don't you just grow up, Richard?' Her voice hardened. 'Take the new start you've been offered. Take the job in America.'

'Or else what?' Richard Heaton growled, obviously realising—at last!—that this situation was well out of his control.

Harrie shrugged. 'I think you may find it's the only decent offer you're going to get. Until a few months ago,' she added less forcefully, 'I believe you were a reporter with scruples.' She looked at the other man challengingly.

She still cared, Quinn realised achingly. And he—he 'cared' for Harrie! He could no longer fight or deny it, to himself at least; he was totally under her spell... And after what Harrie had said to him earlier, about how they would eventually look back on the circumstances of their acquaintance with affection, what good would that do him?

'Jane—' Danie was the one to speak lightly into the telling silence that had followed Harrie's statement '—why don't I take you outside and introduce you to some of the other guests?'

It was made as a polite suggestion, but there was no doubt in anyone's mind—Quinn was sure—that it was nothing of the kind.

'Yes,' the female reporter accepted huskily, obviously intelligent enough to have realised now exactly what was going on. 'Enjoy America, Richard,' came her parting shot as she followed Danie out of the room.

Leaving the three of them, a proudly challenging Harrie, a deeply resentful Richard Heaton, and a tense and angry Quinn, to put an end to this unacceptable situation.

Quinn only hoped Harrie was up to this...

She could do this, Harrie told herself firmly.

It had been a tremendous shock to realise that Richard was actually here at the house, and she had instinctively wondered why he was here. But she needn't have worried; he hadn't come to the house with the intention of expressing undying love for her! Not that she had any feelings of love left towards him, but to think that he might actually have cared for her, after all, might have taken away some of the sting of humiliation she still felt whenever Richard was mentioned.

And he had been mentioned several times by her father in the last few days. Rome had been determined that Richard should be removed from causing any further harm, either to Corinne or herself. And he had acted accordingly...!

But what an idiot she was to have even thought, however briefly, that Richard might actually feel contrite over his actions this last week! One look at his face when she'd entered the sitting-room, seeing him with the blonde-haired woman who had obviously accompanied him, and she had known that Richard had only come here to make more trouble.

She could look at him now quite objectively, and see him for the opportunist he obviously was. He had used Jane Freeman to get himself in here today, in the same way that he had used her in the past.

Yes, she could do this!

'I think that's your cue to leave, Richard,' she told him pointedly once Danie had taken Jane outside.

His expression remained scornfully defiant for several seconds. And then he gave a shrug, his smile rueful. 'I don't suppose it would do any good now to say that I did—do—genuinely care for you?' He raised blond brows.

Harrie heard Quinn's angrily indrawn breath behind her, although she made no effort to turn and look at him. Just what kind of idiot did Quinn think she was? That she would be drawn back in by Richard's charm, that she wouldn't see this was a last-ditch effort on Richard's part to try and retrieve something from the mess he had created? Quinn hadn't come to know her at all this last week if he thought that!

'No, Richard,' she drawled mockingly, even managing a self-derisive smile, 'I don't suppose it would!'

He nodded. 'I don't suppose we'll see each other again, either?'

She quirked her dark eyebrows. 'Not much chance of that once you're based in America.'

It was Richard's turn to smile self-derisively now, shaking his head. 'You know, Harrie, I think I may have underestimated you these last few months,' he said without rancour.

'I think that's a clear possibility,' Harrie nodded, her smile much more genuine now.

'No hard feelings?' Richard prompted softly.

'Eventually…probably not,' she conceded dryly. 'At this particular moment…?' She grinned pointedly.

He gave an acknowledging nod before turning to look at Quinn, who, Harrie realised, had been very quiet the last five minutes or so. Although she doubted that would remain the case for very long!

'I never forget, Heaton. Or forgive,' Quinn told the other man raspingly. 'My advice to you is to stay in America.

An ocean between us may—just may—be enough for me not to have to trouble myself with you again!

And Harrie could see he meant every word of his threat. Luckily, it was obvious that so could Richard!

Although that didn't stop Richard from taking the two steps that separated them, bending down to kiss her lightly on the cheek. 'You're quite a woman, Harrie,' Richard told her admiringly. 'Far too good for me.'

'Well, at least we're in agreement about one thing!' Quinn put in harshly.

Richard turned to the other man with mocking blue eyes. 'I wouldn't look so damn self-satisfied if I were you,' he bit out scornfully. 'Because she's too good for you, too!'

Exactly what did Richard mean by that? Harrie inwardly gasped, avoiding looking directly at Quinn. It was bad enough that she knew she was in love with Quinn, without having a third party allude to the possibility of a relationship between them!

'I think you can safely say that's something else we're in agreement about,' Quinn answered the other man coldly.

Harrie turned to him with widely startled eyes. What on earth did he mean— And then she knew. For Harrie, a relationship that involved her loving someone would ultimately lead to permanence, marriage. To have a husband. But, at thirty-nine, Quinn had obviously never felt the need, so far in his relationships, to legalise anything...! She wasn't 'too good' for Quinn at all, he just had no intention of putting himself in a position where something permanent might be asked of him. Besides, there was Danie...

She straightened proudly. 'Well, at least we now know where we all stand,' she snapped dismissively. 'Now, I really think—'

'Heaton!' her father bit out with dislike as he came rushing into the room, obviously having been informed by

Danie, probably when neither Harrie nor Quinn had come back out onto the patio, that Richard Heaton was in the house. 'If you know what's good for you—'

'He does, Daddy,' Harrie cut in gently, resting a hand lightly on her father's arm.

Rome turned sharply to look at her, and Harrie knew why he did: none of his daughters ever called him 'Daddy' to his face any more. But what he read in Harrie's face seemed to reassure him as Harrie felt some of the tension leaving his body where she still rested her hand on his arm.

'Richard was just leaving—weren't you?' She turned pointedly to the younger man.

Richard gave her a rueful smile. 'I believe I was. But perhaps I'll see you both tomorrow?' he obviously couldn't resist adding mischievously.

'Not me, I'm afraid.' Harrie shook her head. 'I only drew up the contract, someone else will deal with witnessing the signature of it.' There was only so far she was willing to go with this situation—and she had drawn the line at having to see Richard again.

Although this morning rather nullified that decision…!

'I have assistants to deal with such trivialities,' Rome added caustically as Richard looked at him enquiringly.

'In that case…' Richard gave an acknowledging inclination of his head before turning on his heel and walking out of the room, the quiet closing of the front door a few seconds later telling of his departure.

And the tension that filled the room after that departure was not caused by Rome, Harrie freely acknowledged! But the atmosphere that now existed between Quinn and herself was so intense it was impossible for any of them not to be aware of it. Rome looked at the two of them now through narrowed lids.

'I think it's time I was leaving,' Quinn finally rasped.

'But we haven't had brunch yet.' Harrie was aghast as she heard herself make the inconsequential protest. After all, Quinn's departure concerned Danie more now than it did her...

Quinn gave her a scathing glance. 'Somehow I seem to have lost my appetite,' he bit out with distaste.

She swallowed hard. 'In that case, maybe you could offer Richard a lift back into town!' she scorned.

Quinn's eyes became glacial. 'He can crawl the whole damn fifty miles for all I care!' he retorted with disgust before turning to her father. 'I really think it would be better if I left now,' he told the older man flatly.

'Better for whom?' Rome snapped impatiently.

Quinn drew in a harsh breath. 'Me, actually,' he admitted evenly. 'I suddenly find that the country air is too much for me,' he added hardly.

Rome raised blond brows. 'Only the air?' he challenged softly.

'As it happens—no,' Quinn confirmed tautly.

'Quinn—'

'Rome,' Quinn firmly interrupted the other man, his aqua-blue gaze hardening in warning. 'Distance and time are what's needed at the moment, I think.'

'Don't believe that saying about "absence making the heart grow fonder",' Rome rasped harshly. 'It's usually a case of "out of sight, out of mind"!' he added knowingly.

Harrie had been bewildered by their conversation to start with, but now she realised they had to be talking about Danie... God, did everyone know of Quinn's interest in Danie? Rome obviously did—and he approved!

She swallowed hard as the tears came unbidden to her eyes. 'I'll go and tell Danie you're leaving,' she muttered abruptly before hurrying from the room.

When those tears began to fall in earnest.

Quinn and Danie...!

How was she going to bear it?

CHAPTER ELEVEN

'DON'T say a word,' Quinn warned Rome gratingly as he could see the other man was about to do just that.

'But—'

'Not a word, Rome!' Quinn rasped harshly, his eyes glittering a warning too now.

He needed to think. Needed time to work out what to do next. If there was anything he could do next!

Because he loved Harrie Summer. And the thought of leaving here—leaving Harrie!—without at least making her aware of how he felt was beyond all comprehension to him now.

Was this what it was like to be in love with someone? This aching need deep inside him? The knowing that to walk away, to leave her, would be to leave a part of himself—the part of himself that mattered!—behind?

He dropped down heavily into one of the armchairs, staring sightlessly in front of him. He had never known—never realised—that, to love, and not be loved in return, was the most painful thing in the world!

How did people survive this totally helpless feeling? How did they carry on with their normal lives? *If* they did…!

Because at the moment nothing mattered to him but Harrie. Not his sister. Not the bank. Nothing. Certainly not his freedom! And those things, the fabric of his life up to this point in time, the things he'd believed important in his life, had become so much excess baggage since he'd discovered how much he was in love with Harrie…!

He turned dazedly to Rome. 'Is it always like this?'

Rome gave him a sympathetic smile. 'Always,' he confirmed gently. 'Until things are settled. One way or another,' he added softly.

'Hell,' Quinn muttered.

Hell, indeed—to be without that one person who could make those other things mean anything ever again.

Quinn shook his head. 'How on earth did you get through it?' he groaned.

Rome gave a rueful smile. 'It had its compensations!'

'Because yours obviously worked out,' Quinn muttered. 'You married the woman you loved, and had three beautiful daughters with her. But this—this is a damned mess!' he added achingly.

'Only because you've made it so,' Rome told him patiently. 'Oh, not just you,' he conceded as Quinn looked up at him, frowning. 'The two of you—' He broke off as a rather puzzled-looking Danie came back into the room.

'Harrie tells me you're leaving,' she murmured politely.

Quinn gave her a humourless smile. 'Is she outside celebrating?'

'Not that I noticed.' Danie grimaced. 'She was heading off in the direction of the stables as I came in here.'

He frowned. 'What the hell for?'

'She's going out on Ebony, I expect.' Danie shrugged. 'She always does when she has something on her mind.'

Heaton... It had to be seeing Heaton again that had upset Harrie, Quinn realised heavily.

'Rome, exactly what is going on?' It was the blunt Danie who pushed the issue.

Her father shook his head impatiently. 'I've given up even trying to understand,' he muttered.

Danie turned on Quinn, green eyes flashing. 'Have you said or done something to upset Harrie?'

'Me?' he echoed indignantly. 'Has it not occurred to

either of you that Heaton coming here today was more than enough to upset Harrie?'

'Heaton?' Rome repeated in a vaguely dismissive voice.

'Why should that have upset Harrie?' Blunt Danie was once again the one to demand an answer.

Quinn stood up impatiently. 'Are the two of you completely insensitive to—? No, of course you aren't.' He shook his head self-disgustedly; one thing he had learnt this last week, the Summer family were a very close-knit bunch. 'Sorry,' he muttered uncomfortably. 'But of course seeing Heaton again would upset Harrie—'

'Why?' Rome grimaced his puzzlement.

'Because she's in love with the man!' Quinn burst out impatiently, surprised he had to put it into so many words. Both Rome and Danie had to know how hurt Harrie had been by Heaton's behaviour.

'Not that again.' Danie grimaced scornfully. 'Of course Harrie isn't in love with Richard Heaton. How could she be? The man is a total nerd!'

Quinn couldn't help smiling at this apt, if less than grammatical, description of the other man. 'Unfortunately that doesn't preclude someone falling in love with him!'

'It does if that someone is Harrie,' Danie assured him stubbornly.

'If you think of Heaton as a—nerd, what do you think of me?' He looked teasingly at Danie.

'You?' She grinned at him mischievously. 'It's difficult to tell, because at the moment you're so blinded by how you feel about Harrie that you can't see straight,' she told him bluntly. 'But I have a feeling you might just be okay.'

He shook his head, chuckling softly at what he knew, coming from Danie, was a compliment. 'You know, Danie, if I hadn't met Harrie first...!'

She smiled back at him. 'Sorry, Quinn, but you aren't my type.'

'Oh, and just what—?' Quinn broke off abruptly as he saw Rome watching the two of them and frowning. 'We're only joking, Rome,' he told the other man.

'Hmm,' Rome murmured thoughtfully.

'What?' Quinn snapped irritably.

'I know you're joking,' Rome said slowly. 'And the two of you know you are. But it doesn't naturally follow that Harrie knows it too.'

Quinn frowned at the older man. Of course Harrie knew that there was nothing between himself and Danie. It was Harrie that he had kissed. Harrie that he had come here to see. For goodness' sake, Danie spending time with him yesterday evening had just been her taking pity on him.

He had assured Harrie that he hadn't come here to see her! After which he had spent the evening with Danie. And he had been having coffee alone with Danie this morning too when Harrie had returned from her ride.

Could Rome have actually hit upon something...?

Quinn swallowed hard. 'What if you're wrong?'

'What have you got to lose?' Rome challenged.

What had he got to lose?

Yes...what had he got to lose? Hadn't he just realised that he didn't have anything if he couldn't have Harrie?

He drew in a ragged breath. 'Point me in the general direction of the stables?' he requested huskily of Danie.

'I'll do better than that.' She grinned. 'I'll take you as far as the back of the house; you can see the stables from there. And if Harrie won't have you—' she linked her arm lightly through the crook of his as she grinned at him '—come back and we'll go off and have some lunch together somewhere.'

'And to think that until the last couple of days I've been thinking of you as "that bossy redhead"!' he returned mockingly.

'You weren't wrong,' Rome assured him ruefully as he

ave his daughter an affectionate smile. 'The man that
akes on Danie will have a fight on his hands as to "who
vears the trousers"!'

'The "man who takes me on" had better think himself
lamned lucky to have me!' Danie came back with an ar-
ogant wrinkling of her nose.

'Or else!' Rome smiled conspiratorially at Quinn.

He liked this family, Quinn decided as he walked
hrough the house at Danie's side.

But he loved Harrie...!

His smile faded as he thought of the task ahead of him.
Vhat if Harrie rejected him? Worse, laughed in his face...!
Vo, he knew her well enough to realise she wouldn't do
hat. If she turned him down at all, it would be gently.

But, however, it was done, it would still be a turn-
lown...!

'Have you ever accepted defeat, Quinn?' Danie ques-
ioned softly at his side as they reached the courtyard at
he back of the house, the stables, as she had said earlier,
n view now. 'In business? In anything?'

'This is different—'

'No, it isn't,' she assured him. 'The only difference with
his is that you're emotionally involved—'

'That's a hell of a difference, Danie!' he protested
aughingly.

She shrugged. 'My mother always said, "If something's
vorth having"...'

'"It's worth fighting for",' he finished, knowing that to
ave Harrie permanently in his life was worth everything.
You're right, Danie.' He straightened determinedly.
Watch out, Harrie Summer, I'm about to start fighting!'

'But gently,' came Danie's laughing parting shot as he
trode forcefully towards the tables.

Gently, she said, Quinn muttered to himself as he en-
ered the gloom of the stables. He wasn't even sure if

Harrie was still here; she might already have gone out on Ebony.

'Lost your way, Quinn?'

He turned to find Harrie looking at him over the top of a stall, the horse snorting beside her easily recognisable as Ebony. Brought up in the city, Quinn had admired horses from afar, but never been this close to one before. He didn't find the experience any more reassuring than he had as he'd stood at his bedroom window watching as Harrie had ridden away on the back of this monster this morning.

'I was looking for you,' he answered Harrie's opening comment, all the time keeping a wary eye on the snorting Ebony.

Harrie raised dark brows. 'You've found me.' She shrugged.

Quinn frowned. 'I would like to talk to you. But not here,' he added quickly as Ebony stretched his head over the top of his stall to move that snorting nose dangerously close to Quinn. 'I don't think your horse likes me.'

'Of course he does,' Harrie assured him briskly as she let herself out of the stall. 'He would have tried to bite you by now if he didn't!'

Somehow Quinn didn't find that reassuring. But as they moved away from Ebony's stall, it wasn't something he had to worry about.

But what he said to Harrie, now that he was face to face with her, was definitely something to worry about!

'I'm sorry about what happened this morning,' he told her gruffly, noticing that, for all Harrie's outward calm, there was a trace of tears down the paleness of her cheeks. The bastard had made her cry! he realised angrily.

'You mean Richard?' She frowned. 'But that wasn't your fault.'

'No. But—' he grimaced '—I don't like to see you being hurt.'

'No?' Harrie looked at him steadily.

'No!' he confirmed tautly.

'You're missing out on brunch,' she told him huskily.

'So are you,' he pointed out harshly.

She shrugged narrow shoulders. 'I'm not hungry.'

'Neither am I,' he bit out abruptly.

'But your sister and David—'

'I'll see them later,' he dismissed impatiently. 'Harrie, I tried to talk to you earlier this morning—'

'We did talk, Quinn,' she cut in lightly.

'No, we didn't,' he rebuked evenly. 'At least not about anything that matters.'

And he was going to have his say now, if it killed him!

As he had already been told once today—what did he have to lose?

Harrie could feel the tension inside her rising. She didn't want to hear the things Quinn had to say, especially when it involved telling her he now found himself attracted to Danie! Hadn't she made that more than obvious earlier this morning?

'You certainly know how to pick your moments, Quinn,' she taunted lightly, their surroundings far from conducive to any confidences he might want to make concerning Danie.

Although, maybe not... The stables were shadowed, meaning Quinn probably couldn't see her as well as he would be able to if they were outside in the bright sunshine. And there was the added advantage of her being able to escape on Ebony once their conversation was at an end.

'Step into my office, Mr McBride,' she mocked, indicating they should sit down on the bales of hay that were piled in a corner of one of the empty stalls.

Quinn looked far from enamoured at the suggestion,

Harrie noted with amusement as the two of them moved to sit down. He probably didn't want to get hay on his black tailored trousers and blue silk shirt, she acknowledged ruefully. Come to think of it, Quinn had probably never been inside a stable in his life!

The stables were kept meticulously clean, but there was still an aroma of horses and the smells that went along with them. Poor Quinn, she acknowledged ruefully.

'Some office,' he grimaced, looking around them pointedly.

Harrie shrugged. 'I'm a country girl. Maybe not born here, but certainly brought up here. And I love life in the country. One day I intend having a home and stables like this of my own,' she added decidedly.

It had always been her dream. She didn't want to live and work in the city for ever; she'd always hoped that once she married, had children of her own, they would be brought up in the country as she had been. Although, she realised self-derisively, that dream would never have come true if she and Richard had ever decided to make their relationship a permanent one; Richard was definitely a townie, and the work he did would never allow for him living in the country.

Not that Quinn would have been much better, she also acknowledged wistfully. He was as much a town person as Richard had been.

Maybe it was a dream she would have to realise on her own...

'Now what did you want to say?' she prompted Quinn briskly.

He was looking at her searchingly. Although what he hoped to find, Harrie had no idea. She had been upset earlier when she'd left the house, couldn't bear the thought of Quinn and Danie being involved together, but hopefully none of that showed in her face now...?

'Does he really still matter to you that much?' Quinn rasped, letting Harrie know that something certainly did still show on her face.

She frowned. 'Who?'

'Heaton!' Quinn bit out impatiently.

She relaxed slightly. But only slightly. Feeling about Quinn as she did, it wouldn't do to relax too much in his company!

'He doesn't "matter" to me at all,' she dismissed easily.

Quinn shook his head. 'You were upset after he left. And you've been crying,' he added harshly.

Damn, *that* was what showed!

She raised her hands instinctively and smoothed her fingers across the dampness of her cheeks. Those tears certainly hadn't been for Richard!

'I had something in my eye earlier,' she excused.

'Both of them?' Quinn challenged harshly.

She gave an impatient sigh. 'Exactly what is you want from me, Quinn?' she asked, standing up restlessly. 'I've told you I don't care for Richard. I'm not sure that I ever did in the way that you seem to think I did,' she added dismissively; she loved Quinn, damn it—and it was a feeling like nothing else she had ever known before!

Or would ever feel again with anyone else...?

'I've also assured you that you owe me no explanations or apologies yourself just because you've kissed me a couple of times.' She paced up and down the small confines of the stall now. 'What else is it you want?' She rounded on him angrily. 'A blessing on your relationship with Danie? Okay, Quinn, you have it. Now get out of here and let me get on with—' The rest of what she had been going to say was swallowed up as Quinn stood up suddenly, pulling her determinedly into his arms, his mouth coming crashingly down on hers.

Heaven... Oh, God, heaven...!

She'd told herself that she would have to accept that this would never happen again, that she would never again feel the strength of Quinn's arms about her, never know the fierce possession of his mouth against hers.

Never know the hard response of his body as it curved perfectly against hers...?

She wrenched her mouth away from his, looking up at him with glitteringly tear-wet eyes. 'I don't understand...!' she gasped her confusion. How could he respond to her in this way if it were Danie he wanted...?

'We're going to start again, Harrie,' Quinn told her determinedly. 'I'm going to ask you out. You're going to accept,' he bit out firmly. 'We're going to do all those things that other people do when they go out together. And, eventually, in time, you'll forget all about Heaton, and realise that not every man is like him, that some of us—*one* of us,' he added decisively, 'wants you for yourself!'

Now it was Harrie's turn to look searchingly at Quinn. And what she saw there made her breath catch in her throat, her heart leap in her chest. It was true; it was her that Quinn wanted!

'But I thought—you and Danie—'

'I like your sister very much, Harrie,' Quinn cut in dismissively. 'She's blunt, and funny, and—'

'Beautiful,' Harrie put in uncertainly.

'Not as beautiful as you.' Quinn shook his head. 'But even if she were, it would make no difference to how I feel. Can't you see—feel!—that it's you I want?' he groaned impatiently. 'Damn it, not just want, Harrie! I— I—'

She looked at him wonderingly. Because she could see, could feel— 'Quinn...?' she gasped, still not able to believe the emotion she could see in his face.

'I love you, Harrie Summer!' he burst out gratingly.

'Every damned stubborn inch of you! And I wasn't going to tell you that yet, don't want to frighten you off,' he muttered impatiently. 'But it makes no difference,' he added determinedly. 'I am going to ask you out. And you are going to accept!' His arms tightened about her warningly.

Quinn loved her...! Nothing else he had said mattered. Quinn loved her!

She rested her forehead weakly against him. 'I thought it was Danie you were interested in, were going to give "distance and time" to.' She shook he head. 'I couldn't bear it, Quinn. That's the reason I was crying!' She raised her head to look at him. 'You see, Quinn McBride,' she said chokingly, 'I love you, too!'

He looked thunderstruck, holding her at arm's length as he studied her intently.

Harrie looked back at him glowingly. It didn't matter what they had both thought about Richard and Danie. Because they loved each other!

'Say something, Quinn,' she finally laughed chokingly. 'Before I collapse from the tension!'

'I told you once before that if you fall I'll be there to pick you up,' he reminded huskily as he pulled her back against him, his cheek resting against the silkiness of her hair. 'I may not have been willing to admit it, even to myself,' he added self-derisively, 'but I loved you even then. I think I fell in love with you that first day!' he said ruefully.

'You didn't like me very much that day,' she chided lovingly. 'You believed I was Rome's mistress.'

'I was an idiot,' Quinn scorned. 'A jealous one at that. Harrie...' he raised his head to look at her intently '...will you marry me?'

Marry...? Quinn wanted to marry her?

'We'll still go out together,' he told her quickly as she

didn't answer, 'still do all those things other people do when they're getting to know each other. I just—'

'Yes, Quinn,' she burst out breathlessly.

'You'll go out with me?' He looked down at her uncertainly.

She shook her head, smiling glowingly, dark hair tousled down her back. 'I'll marry you,' she corrected huskily. 'Today. Tomorrow. Whenever you want!' she added with certainty. 'I just want to be with you, Quinn. Always,' she told him firmly.

He swallowed hard. 'A banker isn't going to be too boring for you?'

'In comparison with what?' She frowned her puzzlement.

Quinn shrugged. 'A film producer sounds rather more exciting—' He broke off as Harrie put her fingers firmly over his lips. 'No?' he prompted uncertainly.

'Most definitely not,' she assured him laughingly, knowing he had to be talking about Adam. How stupid they had been, jealous of other people in their uncertainty of loving each other! 'I doubt Adam will ever settle down with one woman,' she dismissed. 'And even if he does, it most certainly won't be me! I'm ashamed to say I used Adam as a shield last night. In the same way I now believe you used Danie…?'

'Guilty, I'm afraid.' Quinn sighed. 'Although Danie mischievously went along with it,' he added ruefully. 'I think she wanted to see what your reaction would be.'

'She would,' Harrie acknowledged affectionately. 'She didn't like the fact that I was less than honest with her about my being in love with you.'

Quinn nodded. 'She thinks we're both stubbornly uncooperative on that score,' he confirmed ruefully.

'I think what my sister needs is a man of her own. But it won't be you!' Harrie added with a possessiveness of her own. 'You're the man *I* love, Quinn,' she added seriously. 'The man I want to spend the rest of my life with,' she told him shyly. 'And I don't want to spend weeks or months "going out together",' she assured him determinedly. 'I want us to be together now. In fact...' She groaned her physical as well as emotional need of him as the two of them sank to the hay-strewn floor.

Quinn's arms tightened about her as they lay together. 'You don't think Ebony will be too jealous?' he teased emotionally.

'I don't care how anyone else feels about us being together, Quinn,' she assured him confidently. 'Although I have a feeling Rome approves of you...!' she added affectionately. If her father hadn't liked and respected Quinn, then she knew the younger man would never have been invited back here.

Quinn laughed huskily. 'He may not feel quite so approving if I bring his beloved eldest daughter back to the house with bits of straw sticking out of her hair from where I've obviously ravished her in the stables!'

Harrie curved her arm up about his neck as she slowly pulled him down to her. 'Then we had better make sure we dispose of the straw before we go back,' she murmured longingly. 'Hadn't we...?'

Quinn looked down at her intently. 'I do love you, Harrie. So very much.'

And it obviously wasn't an emotion he found it easy to admit to. But then, neither did she. The joy of it all was, despite what they might have thought otherwise, that the love they felt was for each other...!

'And I love you, Quinn McBride,' she told him huskily before their mouths fused together.

Harrie McBride. Yes, she liked the sound of that.

But not as much as she loved Quinn McBride...

EPILOGUE

'SO TELL me,' drawled the husky voice of Gypsy Rosa as she gazed down into the palm of his hand, 'what happened after you met your tall, dark, beautiful stranger?'

Quinn grinned as he lay beside her in the bed. 'I married her, of course!'

Of course... They both knew there had been no 'of course' about their brief and tempestuous courtship. It still brought him out in a cold sweat every time he thought about how nearly he and Harrie had walked away from each other, each believing the other was in love with someone else.

'Hey, I was only joking!' Harrie snuggled down against him. 'Of course you married her—I would have been very disappointed if you hadn't!'

Quinn's arms remained firmly about her as he held her close to him. The two of them had been married for three weeks now—three weeks of pure heaven as far as he was concerned—and he still found it hard to believe Harrie returned his love as fiercely as he loved her.

They had been married by special licence only five days after realising they were in love with each other, and the following three weeks had been the happiest Quinn had ever known. Looking back on his life before Harrie, it seemed bleak and empty; in fact, he wondered why he'd ever fought against his love for her. It was like a tidal wave, washing him off his feet—and he didn't care if he never went back on dry land ever again!

'We'll have to get up soon, my darling.' Harrie stretched sensually beside him. 'Danie is coming for lunch today.'

Quinn laughed huskily. 'It won't be the first time she's arrived here and found us still in bed!' On one memorable occasion, it had been five o'clock in the afternoon!

Being part of the Summer family was as warm with belonging as he had thought it would be. Rome had been obviously more than pleased to see his eldest daughter married to someone he liked and respected, and Danie and Andie—he had finally met her at the wedding!—treated him much like the big brother he was to Corinne.

Life was good, he realised. More than good. With Harrie at his side, as his wife, it was perfect...!

Harrie moved to look down lovingly at her husband. 'I thought we might make an effort today,' she said indulgently. 'Danie is going to think we're always in bed together!'

Quinn quirked one dark brow. 'And aren't we?'

She laughed softly. 'Yes,' she conceded ruefully.

Having Quinn as her husband was like nothing she could ever have imagined, their love for each other all-consuming, meaning they resented anything, or anyone, that took them away from each other.

In fact, after making what she had taken at the time to be a disparaging remark about 'never having her work for him'—a remark he had since explained really meant he couldn't see himself getting any work done if she were that close to him!—she now spent a considerable amount of time at the bank assisting Quinn on legal matters. Much to her father's irritation!

'Do you think—?' She broke off as the telephone beside the bed began to ring.

'With any luck, that's Danie calling to say she can't make it,' Quinn murmured hopefully.

'Naughty!' Harrie chided lovingly even as she reached over and picked up the receiver.

She listened patiently as Danie spoke economically on the other end of the line. 'That's okay, Danie,' she assured once her sister had finished talking. 'We'll see you later in the week,' she told Danie warmly before ringing off.

'There is a God, after all!' Quinn unashamedly showed his approval of Danie's obvious inability to make it here for lunch.

Harrie laughed huskily even as she snuggled back down into his arms. 'She has to go somewhere for Rome,' she dismissed lightly. 'Now, Mr McBride, what were you saying about staying in bed...?' She looked up at him mischievously.

'I was saying—Mrs McBride—' he rolled over in the bed, curving her body into his '—now that Danie won't be here for lunch, that I see absolutely no reason to get out of bed at all today!'

'We could starve.' Harrie chuckled.

'What a way to go!' Quinn murmured even as his mouth came down possessively on hers.

What a way, indeed...!

HARLEQUIN Presents
Passion™

Looking for stories that **sizzle**?

Wanting a read that has a little extra **spice**?

Harlequin Presents® is thrilled to bring you romances that turn up the **heat!**

Every other month there'll be a **PRESENTS PASSION™** book by one of your favorite authors.

Don't miss
THE ARABIAN MISTRESS
by **Lynne Graham**
On-sale June 2001, Harlequin Presents® #2182

and look out for
THE HOT-BLOODED GROOM
by **Emma Darcy**
On-sale August 2001, Harlequin Presents® #2195

Pick up a **PRESENTS PASSION™** novel—
where **seduction** is guaranteed!

Available wherever Harlequin books are sold.

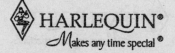

HARLEQUIN®
Makes any time special ®

Visit us at www.eHarlequin.com

HPPASSB

*Harlequin truly does
make any time special....
This year we are celebrating
weddings in style!*

A
Walk
Down
the Aisle

WEDDING CELEBRATION

To help us celebrate, we want you to tell us how wearing the
Harlequin wedding gown will make your wedding day special. As
the grand prize, Harlequin will offer one lucky bride the chance to
"Walk Down the Aisle" in the Harlequin wedding gown!

There's more...

For her honeymoon, she and her groom will spend five nights at the
Hyatt Regency Maui. As part of this five-night honeymoon at the
hotel renowned for its romantic attractions, the couple will enjoy a candlelit
dinner for two in Swan Court, a sunset sail on the hotel's catamaran, and
duet spa treatments.

A HYATT RESORT AND SPA   Maui • Molokai • Lanai

To enter, please write, in, 250 words or less, how wearing the Harlequin
wedding gown will make your wedding day special. The entry will be
judged based on its emotionally compelling nature, its originality and
creativity, and its sincerity. This contest is open to Canadian and U.S.
residents only and to those who are 18 years of age and older. There is no
purchase necessary to enter. Void where prohibited. See further contest
rules attached. Please send your entry to:

Walk Down the Aisle Contest

In Canada	In U.S.A.
P.O. Box 637	P.O. Box 9076
Fort Erie, Ontario	3010 Walden Ave.
L2A 5X3	Buffalo, NY 14269-9076

You can also enter by visiting www.eHarlequin.com
Win the Harlequin wedding gown and the vacation of a lifetime!
The deadline for entries is October 1, 2001.

HARLEQUIN®
Makes any time special®

PHWDACONT1

HARLEQUIN WALK DOWN THE AISLE TO MAUI CONTEST 1197
OFFICIAL RULES
NO PURCHASE NECESSARY TO ENTER

1. To enter, follow directions published in the offer to which you are responding. Contest begins April 2, 2001, and ends on October 1, 2001. Method of entry may vary. Mailed entries must be postmarked by October 1, 2001, and received by October 8, 2001.

2. Contest entry may be, at times, presented via the Internet, but will be restricted solely to residents of certain geographic areas that are disclosed on the Web site. To enter via the Internet, if permissible, access the Harlequin Web site (www.eHarlequin.com) and follow the directions displayed online. Online entries must be received by 11:59 p.m. E.S.T. on October 1, 2001.

   In lieu of submitting an entry online, enter by mail by hand-printing (or typing) on an 8½" x 11" plain piece of paper, your name, address (including zip code), Contest number/name and in 250 words or fewer, why winning a Harlequin wedding dress would make your wedding day special. Mail via first-class mail to: Harlequin Walk Down the Aisle Contest 1197, (in the U.S.) P.O. Box 9076, 3010 Walden Avenue, Buffalo, NY 14269-9076, (in Canada) P.O. Box 637, Fort Erie, Ontario L2A 5X3, Cana

   Limit one entry per person, household address and e-mail address. Online and/or mailed entries received from persons residing in geographic areas in which Internet entry is not permissible will be disqualified.

3. Contests will be judged by a panel of members of the Harlequin editorial, marketing and public relations staff based on the following criteria:

   * Originality and Creativity—50%
   * Emotionally Compelling—25%
   * Sincerity—25%

   In the event of a tie, duplicate prizes will be awarded. Decisions of the judges are final.

4. All entries become the property of Torstar Corp. and will not be returned. No responsibility is assumed for lost, late, illegible incomplete, inaccurate, nondelivered or misdirected mail or misdirected e-mail, for technical, hardware or software failures o any kind, lost or unavailable network connections, or failed, incomplete, garbled or delayed computer transmission or any human error which may occur in the receipt or processing of the entries in this Contest.

5. Contest open only to residents of the U.S. (except Puerto Rico) and Canada, who are 18 years of age or older, and is void wherever prohibited by law; all applicable laws and regulations apply. Any litigation within the Province of Quebec respecting the conduct or organization of a publicity contest may be submitted to the Régie des alcools, des courses et des jeux for a ruling. Any litigation respecting the awarding of a prize may be submitted to the Régie des alcools, des courses et des jeux o for the purpose of helping the parties reach a settlement. Employees and immediate family members of Torstar Corp. and D. L. Blair, Inc., their affiliates, subsidiaries and all other agencies, entities and persons connected with the use, marketing o conduct of this Contest are not eligible to enter. Taxes on prizes are the sole responsibility of winners. Acceptance of any pri offered constitutes permission to use winner's name, photograph or other likeness for the purposes of advertising, trade and promotion on behalf of Torstar Corp., its affiliates and subsidiaries without further compensation to the winner, unless prohibited by law.

6. Winners will be determined no later than November 15, 2001, and will be notified by mail. Winners will be required to sign a return and Affidavit of Eligibility form within 15 days after winner notification. Noncompliance within that time period may resu in disqualification and an alternative winner may be selected. Winners of trip must execute a Release of Liability prior to ticke and must possess required travel documents (e.g. passport, photo ID) where applicable. Trip must be completed by Novembe 2002. No substitution of prize permitted by winner. Torstar Corp. and D. L. Blair, Inc., their parents, affiliates, and subsidiarie are not responsible for errors in printing or electronic presentation of Contest, entries and/or game pieces. In the event of printing or other errors which may result in unintended prize values or duplication of prizes, all affected game pieces or entrie shall be null and void. If for any reason the Internet portion of the Contest is not capable of running as planned, including infection by computer virus, bugs, tampering, unauthorized intervention, fraud, technical failures, or any other causes beyond the control of Torstar Corp. which corrupt or affect the administration, secrecy, fairness, integrity or proper conduct of the Contest, Torstar Corp. reserves the right, at its sole discretion, to disqualify any individual who tampers with the entry proces and to cancel, terminate, modify or suspend the Contest or the Internet portion thereof. In the event of a dispute regarding an online entry, the entry will be deemed submitted by the authorized holder of the e-mail account submitted at the time of entry. Authorized account holder is defined as the natural person who is assigned to an e-mail address by an Internet access provid online service provider or other organization that is responsible for arranging e-mail address for the domain associated with t submitted e-mail address. **Purchase or acceptance of a product offer does not improve your chances of winnin**

7. Prizes: (1) Grand Prize—A Harlequin wedding dress (approximate retail value: $3,500) and a 5-night/6-day honeymoon trip Maui, Hi, including round-trip air transportation provided by Maui Visitors Bureau from Los Angeles International Airport (winner is responsible for transportation to and from Los Angeles International Airport) and a Harlequin Romance Package, including hotel accomodations (double occupancy) at the Hyatt Regency Maui Resort and Spa, dinner for (2) two at Swan Court, a sunset sail on Kiele V and a spa treatment for the winner (approximate retail value: $4,000); (5) Five runner-up prize of a $1000 gift certificate to selected retail outlets to be determined by Sponsor (retail value $1000 ea.). Prizes consist of onl those items listed as part of the prize. Limit one prize per person. All prizes are valued in U.S. currency.

8. For a list of winners (available after December 17, 2001) send a self-addressed, stamped envelope to: Harlequin Walk Down Aisle Contest 1197 Winners, P.O. Box 4200 Blair, NE 68009-4200 or you may access the www.eHarlequin.com Web site through January 15, 2002.

Contest sponsored by Torstar Corp., P.O. Box 9042, Buffalo, NY 14269-9042, U.S.A.

PHWDACONT2

If you enjoyed what you just read,
then we've got an offer you can't resist!

Take 2 bestselling
love stories FREE!
Plus get a FREE surprise gift!

Clip this page and mail it to Harlequin Reader Service®

IN U.S.A.	IN CANADA
3010 Walden Ave.	P.O. Box 609
P.O. Box 1867	Fort Erie, Ontario
Buffalo, N.Y. 14240-1867	L2A 5X3

YES! Please send me 2 free Harlequin Presents® novels and my free surprise gift. After receiving them, if I don't wish to receive anymore, I can return the shipping statement marked cancel. If I don't cancel, I will receive 6 brand-new novels every month, before they're available in stores! In the U.S.A., bill me at the bargain price of $3.34 plus 25¢ shipping & handling per book and applicable sales tax, if any*. In Canada, bill me at the bargain price of $3.74 plus 25¢ shipping & handling per book and applicable taxes**. That's the complete price and a savings of at least 10% off the cover prices—what a great deal! I understand that accepting the 2 free books and gift places me under no obligation ever to buy any books. I can always return a shipment and cancel at any time. Even if I never buy another book from Harlequin, the 2 free books and gift are mine to keep forever.

106 HEN DFNY
306 HEN DC7T

Name	(PLEASE PRINT)	
Address	Apt.#	
City	State/Prov.	Zip/Postal Code

* Terms and prices subject to change without notice. Sales tax applicable in N.Y.
** Canadian residents will be charged applicable provincial taxes and GST.
  All orders subject to approval. Offer limited to one per household and not valid to
  current Harlequin Presents® subscribers..
  ® are registered trademarks of Harlequin Enterprises Limited.

PRES01   ©2001 Harlequin Enterprises Limited